MW00568000

TRUE LIES The Book of Bad Advice

TRUE LIES The Book of Bad Advice

By Mariko Tamaki

WOMEN'S PRESS | TORONTO

TRUE LIES: The Book of Bad Advice
Mariko Tamaki

The first paperback edition published in 2002 by
Women's Press
180 Bloor Street West, Suite 1202
Toronto, Ontario
M5S 2V6

www.womenspress.ca

Women's Press acknowledges the financial support of the
Government of Canada through the Book Publishing Industry
Development Programme for our publishing activities.

NATIONAL LIBRARY OF CANADA CATALOGUING IN PUBLICATION DATA

Tamaki, Mariko
  True lies : the book of bad advice / Mariko Tamaki.

Collection of short monologues.
ISBN 0-88961-402-4

I. Title.

PS8589.A768T78 2002   C811'.6   C2002-901770-X
PR9199.4.T34T78 2002

COVER & BOOK DESIGN Zab Design & Typography
AUTHOR PHOTOGRAPHY R. Kelly Clipperton

02   03   04   05   06   07   08   7   6   5   4   3   2   1

Printed and bound in Canada by Transcontinental Printing

for ma and pa

 Contents

ACKNOWLEDGEMENTS

The stories in this book would not have been written if I had not first had somewhere to read them. Every piece hit the stage before I ever thought it would end up in a book. This would not have happened without the tireless dedication of all the sexy women and men who have organized readings, open mikes, and cabarets in Toronto and Montreal. Thank you to the organizers of Girl Spit (Zoe Whittall), Clit Lit (Elizabeth Ruth), Cheap Queers (The Hard Workin' Homosexuals), Fruitloops (Supporting Our Youth), Fem Cab (Nightwood Theatre), Jerk Off! (the Come as You Are Collective), and Strange Sisters (Buddies In Bad

Times Theatre). Thanks also to the Toronto Women's Bookstore and This Ain't The Rosedale Library (both good places to read and sell your books).

Thank you to Sam Hiyate and Jenny Bullough for all their help and support at the beginning of this project. All my love to everyone at Women's Press, who last year decided that they would make this book happen, and be really-really sweet to me in the process. Thank you to Abi Slone and Zoe Whittall who have been my unpaid editors and support system for over six years. I could never appreciate you enough. Some day I'm going to pay you back with mountains of fabulous shoes.

Everything I write is dedicated to my parents, who refuse to cause me grievous physical injury, despite all the things I may or may not have written about them. Nothing in this book should make you think they are anything but amazing, incredibly patient people.

Last but not least, thank you to Lisa Ayuso, who is both my partner in crime and my most precious muffin.

Thanks to you too, honey.

xx mariko

My friends, out of a sense of concern for their implied reputations and my so-called credibility, say I should tell you that not all of my stories happened the way I say they did. In my defence, I don't think I ever implied that they did, but I guess there is such a thing as guilt by omission.

If it makes them feel better, I have no problem admitting that I am a liar at heart.

It's true.

I am.

The truth is that it's always been easier for me to tell a lie than the truth. My grandmother told me once that lies are like bubble gum, they stick to your teeth and if you swallow them, they take twelve years to digest. My grandmother says that truth is like honey, sweet on your tongue.

Oh if only it were true.

I think I would be more inclined to compare lies to pearls; they look better strung together in a set.

Ever since I was wee I've tended to take a kind of windy, twisty-road approach to storytelling in all forms. I find it easier to communicate when I don't have to stick to the facts, when I can switch things around so they're easier for me to say, adding details that I think sound better. I don't see anything wrong with tweaking the facts if it makes things more interesting or amusing. I tell people that that's why they call it telling a story and not telling the truth. You can call it lying if you want. Especially if it's you that's ended up in one of these stories.

TRUE LIES The Book of Bad Advice

A Tawdry Dukes
of Hazzard Tale

ACCORDING TO ME and my friends, there are lots of reasons for a person to masturbate. Sometimes we masturbate because we're bored, sometimes it's for money, and sometimes, well, a quiet spot in Eglinton Park is too sweet to resist. If I were asked to recall all the places where I have masturbated in my life, I would probably have a mental meltdown. It would be like asking a vacuum cleaner salesperson to recall every hotel room he's slept in. The frequency of my self-pleasuring is so great, in fact, that the only masturbatory event I can still remember with keen accuracy is the night I first touched down. It was, I recall, the result of a lethal mix of the word *molester* and the cunning good looks of Tom Wopat, also known as Luke Duke, star of *The Dukes of Hazzard.*

I can't be sure where I first heard the word *molester.* This was the eighties, so it could have been on TV or something, like on *The Equalizer* maybe. It's more likely that I first heard it from my parents, who at the time were bent on the idea of making me *street smart.* This was, of course, before Toronto's infamous Alison Parrott, who was supposed to be street smart, went downtown to get a track-and-field photograph taken and never returned. At the time, uptown Toronto kids like myself were considered safe, so long as we had no intent of getting into the cars of any strange men.

My father was and is a real minimalist, so our talks mostly consisted of basic commandments.

He'd say something like, "Don't get into any strange cars."

And I'd say, "Why?"

And he'd say, "Do you know what a *molester* is?"

And I'd perk up and say, "No!"

And then he'd pause and six minutes later he'd look at me again and say, "Don't get into any strange cars."

A lack of information fuelled the wheels of my imagination. If I look back, I think every little bit of information my parents didn't tell me led to some sort of sick obsession. You can take that to mean whatever you want.

Needless to say, shortly after this conversation the word *molester* became my favourite word.

One night, lying on my princess canopy bed, shortly after watching a particularly stunning episode of *The Dukes of Hazzard*, it suddenly occurred to me that Luke Duke, who was clearly the darker and stockier of the Dukes, could possibly BE A MOLESTER. This realization could have had something to do with the fact that he was the more brooding of the two and he had access to the CAR, which, I gathered, was an important element of molesting activities. I briefly considered the likelihood that molesting involved sliding around ON the car, since that's what Luke seemed to enjoy doing. I cannot even begin to tell you how excited I was by this idea. I was having little hot flashes. Clearly I found the prospect of being molested by Luke Duke *extremely alluring*. I didn't even know what alluring was, and I found it alluring. I lay in bed in the dark for hours, thinking about being molested. I was very inventive. I found a million uses for the car that didn't have doors that opened. When I thought up a fantasy that I found particularly enjoyable, I reached for my Care Bear.

Incidentally, I don't know if any of you have ever masturbated with your Care Bear while dreaming of the strong, grease-stained hands of Luke Duke. As far as I am concerned it's an activity that Martha Stewart's "good things" have sorely overlooked. I think it's sad how often the sexual prowess of the average stuffed animal is dismissed.

For some time after this hump session the word *molester*

stuck in the back of my head, interrupting my thoughts on a regular basis. I stared intently at the people around me, waiting for the right time and person to tell my heavy word. I was sure that if I didn't get it off my chest it would burn a hole right through me. So I told my friend Sarah one day while we were playing "horses."

"What kind of horse are you?" Sarah asked.

"I'm a molester." I said. "I'm a palomino."

Sarah, who was obviously not street smart, shrugged. "Does that make you a boy palomino or a girl?"

"A boy."

And just like that, I was a molester for the rest of the day, happily rocking on my invisible horse with visions of *The Dukes of Hazzard* dancing through my head.

Later that evening my mother came into my room. It was to be the first of many evenings my mother would come into my room looking that particular shade of weirdly pissed-off pale.

"Did you tell Sarah you were a molester?" she asked.

"Yes," I said.

I feel I should note at this point in my sad story that this particular exchange is a textbook example of why I turned out to be the fucked up person I am today. As my mother sat on my bed, holding the hand of her disgusting and twisted daughter, my father leaned in the doorway giggling.

"You were a molester horse?" he asked.

"Yes," I said. "From *The Dukes of Hazzard.*"

"Oh," my father said, "so what kind of horse is that?"

"A palomino."

My father bent over and scurried out of the room laughing hysterically. This was not the first time I had seen my father do this. The first time involved a note I had left for my parents on the dinner table expressing my desire for my parents to buy me new jazz tights.

MUST HAVE **BLACK TITS** BY TOMORROW, it said.

My father still has the sign in his office.

Anyhow, soon after my father took his leave, my mother, looking incredibly concerned, took my hand and squeezed it like an old tube of toothpaste.

"MOLESTERS," she said, in a very quiet and concerned voice, "are horrible, horrible people. YOU DO NOT want to be a molester. Do you understand me?"

"Yes," I said.

"And I never ever want to hear you say that word again, unless someone has done something very, very bad to you. Then you tell mommy or daddy, okay?"

"Okay."

"Ever again."

"Okay."

The next day at school Sarah told me her mother had said I was sick and she shouldn't play with me if I was going to use bad words. I explained that my mother had told me never to say the word again anyway. If I was to say the word again, I advised myself, I certainly wouldn't say it in front of Sarah, who was obviously a snitch. If my recent experience had taught me anything, it was don't talk to your parents about what you do in the backyard and don't be a molester.

For these reasons I will not be divulging the details of the other game that I later invented: IF MICHAEL JACKSON WERE HERE, RIGHT NOW, AND HE WERE NAKED, WHAT WOULD YOU DO TO HIM?

The Games We Play

AT THE URGING of a heterosexual friend of mine, who is always clipping articles on relationships for me, since that's what I seem to want to write about, I recently read an article about a therapist who reunites distanced couples using role-play. According to Dr. Leemon, a well-paid New York professional, the best way to rediscover the roots of your relationship is to re-enact basic male/female roles in proactive re-creations of common couples' interactive scenarios, or "games." This, apparently, is supposed to help you achieve some sort of understanding of the core elements of your relationship, what Leemon calls "the keys to the union," which sounds vaguely municipal to me.

When I heard this, I wondered: what kind of games, exactly, would this therapy require you to play? The first thing that came to my mind was this game we used to play in grade two where a group of grade four boys would chase and tag girls in the schoolyard, pinning them to the ground and snapping the elastic bands of their underwear. I can sort of see how you could fall in love again playing that game, but then you'd have to sit around and pick the gravel out of the scrapes on your knees, which is probably way less cool when you're forty as opposed to four.

Maybe they just make you sit around and play house with little plastic ovens and little plastic briefcases, screaming, "HONEY, I'M HOME!"

Though I can't imagine myself ever paying for this particular kind of therapy, I can see the value in actually distilling relations between the sexes (whatever they may be) down to a matter of "games." I've always considered it a "joke," but "game" works as well, I think, especially if you consider the advantages of knowing the rules, and knowing how to win.

So in honour of Dr. Leemon and everyone who likes to play games, here are a few games that I remember.

THE GAME Tea
LEVEL 1
AGES Toddler and up

PARTICIPANTS Beginners who, having mastered the art of sitting up, must now master the art of sitting up and being nice (to other people).

SET-UP Baby 1 and Baby 2 are placed within vicinity of cups and saucers and "tea." Dress-up clothes may also be required. Since gender difference is not really noted at this stage of the game, gender difference between babies is a moot point.

HOW TO PLAY Babies 1 and 2 sit up and sip invisible tea, also known as "pretend" tea. As participants become more mature, conversation may be added to this set-up.

DURATION Roughly the attention span of the average toddler, four minutes, five minutes tops.

THE WINNER Whoever is left at the table, or, alternatively, whoever first realizes that there's no such thing as "pretend" tea.

THE GAME Sheep Eyes
LEVEL 4
AGES 4 and up

PARTICIPANTS Girls with a healthy imagination, an hour to kill before dinner, and little to no understanding of human biology.

SET-UP Girl 1 and Girl 2 pretend to be two animals and/or celebrities falling in love. Note: Since game is not based in the real world (no understanding of biology), animals need not be of the same species or even in any way compatible. A popular combination is a wolf (Girl 1) and a unicorn (Girl 2). Other possible combinations: bull and golden retriever; Michael Jackson and Siamese cat; hamster and snake.

HOW TO PLAY Wolf falls in love with unicorn. To demonstrate this, wolf, Girl 1, makes "sheep eyes" (or stolen glances) until these are noticed and finally acknowledged by unicorn Girl 2. Eventually, wolf and unicorn end up going on a date (possible locations for date: enchanted forest, waterfall). At end of date unicorn and wolf decide to marry and mate shortly thereafter (note: no understanding of human biology). Mating lasts about ten seconds (okay, maybe a little understanding of biology). After delivery of children (by either mate), unicorn and wolf cease sexual relations and watch *Three's Company*.

DURATION OF GAME Average two to three hours depending on weather and amount of time before *The Dukes of Hazzard*.

THE WINNER Whoever doesn't have to give birth.

THE GAME High School Dance
LEVEL 7–13
AGES 13 to graduation

PARTICIPANTS High school teens (in this context, my context, private school teens)

SET-UP Roughly 150 teens congregate in a high school

auditorium after consuming various amounts of alcohol (note presence of top 40 hits as well as tried-and-true classics such as "Wild Thing," "Stairway to Heaven," and "Mony, Mony"). Within this crowd: 1 boy and 1 girl (it's a hetero game).

HOW TO PLAY Trying to look disinterested and yet somehow willing and available, girl and boy will dance in slowly shrinking circles until slow dance. If all goes well, girl and boy kiss. If kiss becomes "make-out session," players are invited to continue to try for one or all of various other possible activities including outside-the-school grope, movie-theatre grope, long-lasting relationship, prom. *

DURATION Anywhere from two minutes to a year to a wedding.

THE WINNER Whoever gets the best kisser, whoever ends up with the best dancer, whoever ends up not having to pay to see a movie that year.

THE GAME Coffee, also known as "Wanna go for coffee?"
LEVEL Highest, extreme difficulty
AGES 17 and up

PARTICIPANTS So-called "adults" who are "single," or at least appear to be so.

SET-UP Urban setting. Girl/Boy 1 and Girl/Boy 2 meet somehow, somewhere, and agree, after exchanging phone numbers, to meet for coffee.

How To Play: Girl/Boy 1 and Girl/Boy 2, who may or may not be falling in love, go for coffee (1 asks 2 or 2 asks 1, no biggie). Note that elements from games at all levels come into play here: participants are expected to be able to sit upright and be "nice," and a certain amount of pretending is also helpful although real tea, or coffee, will be used. An understanding of the art of stolen glances will also be extremely useful, although unlike "Sheep Eyes," this game will hopefully require a more detailed understanding of human biology. The ability to kiss and dance might also come into play; keep these skills on reserve.

The goal of this game is to figure out, as soon as possible, whether or not both players are playing. Coffee is not a game of "how" but of "what." As in, "Are we having coffee or are we *having* coffee?" Outside players may be used as an assist, but be careful you don't put someone else into play because you don't know what you're doing. A kiss may be required. Embarrassment risk factor is definitely high; definitely much higher than pretend tea.

DURATION Two coffees to fuckin' forever.

THE WINNER Whoever ends up (in my context) on top.

Incidentally, if there is someone out there who's tired of playing games, let me know.

Reasons to
Give a Blow Job

(Know, before you read this, that the following list is just a preamble to my favourite blow job story.)

All in all, there are four reasons to give a guy a blow job.

1 MONEY Money, as I see it, is a good reason to do a good many things. There are a lot of things I've recently realized I'd do for money and I don't see anything wrong with that. If you want to do it, even if you only want to do it for money, you should be allowed to. If someone offered me

$200 and a little respect, I think, in a certain situation, I would give a blow job. I would warn the person, though, that the majority of my experience with blow jobs comes from watching, rather than doing, so I'm guessing I'd be pretty bad at it. If I were good at it, I think I'd probably charge more. Or ask for a car or something.

2 POSSIBLE RECIPROCATION

Sometimes it's an "I'll scratch your back, you scratch mine" kind of world and you've got to give a little to get a little. Completely fair, so long as both parties keep up their end of the bargain and no one gets "tired" before they can finish the job. It's too bad you can't take back a blow job in cases where the reciprocation proves disappointing. If you could, there are two blow jobs I would take back right now.

3 HOMOSEXUALITY

Of the fifteen friends I have who love sucking cock, fourteen are gay. Part of me used to think this was all about showing off. Like, "I like sucking cock 'cause I'm good at it 'cause I practice at home." My friend Chris says gay people like sucking cock because they're so giving — except he won't lend me his New Order CD and he threw up on the porch on my birthday. Not so giving.

4 BRAGGER'S RIGHTS

The best part of any sexual adventure is the re-telling.

A couple nights ago at a party that was dying a predictable and yet horrible death, the evening was saved when the hostess's best friend piped in with a suggestion worthy of a second beer and another pizza. "Let's tell blow job stories," she said. It was a lesbian party so everyone sat down and dug their heels in. Campfire time. I love it when things like that happen, when a mixture of boredom, just a little booze, and a fear of silence bring out the juicy gossip and slight exaggerations. It's the stuff of dreams for me. Just so you know: if you see me at one of these parties and I hear your story, I have full rights to reprint it at will as my own.

Just so you know.

In my humble opinion there are four things that make a blow job story interesting: location, age, dick shape and size, and the money shot. If at least one of these elements isn't notable, what you have is not a blow job story, but a blow job. Taking these points into consideration, I have a sum total of one blow job story. I didn't get to tell it that night because I got a little trashed and passed out before the story circle got to me. I always get trashed at lesbo potlucks because they're really boring and I can't eat the food because it's vegan; gives me the runs.

So I'm going to tell it here today instead because honestly, since I've never received any of the other above-listed benefits of a blow job, I might as well receive this one.

Here it is. One of the first blow jobs I gave happened on a one night stand. It was purely a peer-pressure blow job, which took place as the result of an exchange at summer school — specifically an argument I got into which revealed that I didn't know what semen tasted like. I guessed and said it tasted sweet and was immediately busted.

As fate would have it, on my way home that very day I ran into an old grade school sweetheart whom I had once kissed at a dance. He asked me out and I, gleefully rubbing my hands together, accepted.

What use is a good boy if he can't get you through a little peer pressure anyway?

As it turned out, unfortunately, Dave was one of those strange boys who was less interested in sexual adventures than he was in an intimate and meaningful relationship. Dave's mom, I guessed, spent an excess of quality time with him. Either that or she completely ignored him. Blissfully unaware of my plans to attack his groin area when he wasn't looking, Dave carried on with his none too obvious plan to be the best date ever. He opened every door, paid for the movie, and talked my ear off all night. At eleven o'clock, as he walked me home, I finally pushed him into the kiddy park a block from my house and with a breathless whisper offered my services.

He could hardly turn me down, as my sleeve was stuck in his zipper. Uneducated and overeager, I whipped him out and attempted to swallow him whole, digging my knees into the cold grass as I braced my arms and tried to make my jaw relax as much as humanly possible. I had absolutely nothing to go on, having seen little porn at that age, and hoped some sort of genetic code would kick

31

in that would show me how this longish, fleshy thing worked.

Unfortunately, biology did not come through and I was soon choking as Dave's penis jabbed me in the back of the throat. There's nothing less cool than trying to hide from your blow job-ee the fact that you're choking. I struggled for several minutes before a frightened Dave pitched his left hand in and helped me finish the job. For my efforts I got an eyeful of spunk. Just so you know, boys, spunk really stings. After Dave ran off, I practically had to crawl home. I stuck my head in a sink full of water until I got my eyesight back.

That Monday at summer school I went up to my friend Mary with a triumphant smile. "It tastes like old rubber tires," I said.

"Either that," said Mary, "or chicken soup."

"Don't get it in your eyes though."

"Yeah, I know."

Shortly after this BJ, I would renounce my availability for a different method of dining out. Dave, who "fell in love with me" shortly after the BJ, still gets very excited on the odd occasion that I see him. I think he thinks that the mere sight of him makes me want to suck dick. This, I have to tell you, couldn't be farther from the truth. I'm nice to him though, because it's a really great story (I think) and I wouldn't have it in my arsenal without him. Plus now I know what guys taste like, one guy at least, and you've got to think that's worth something.

Incidentally, in case you're curious, I have, in my longer career with women, never tasted a woman who tasted like any kind of soup. I hope I never do.

Listen Without Prejudice

BEFORE ANYONE DECIDES to be my friend, the first thing they need to know about me is that I am a woman without faith. Despite the fact that I am extremely superstitious, and despite the fact that I have a collection of hologram Jesus postcards in my kitchen, when it comes to matters and practices relating to any sort of religion, I am predictably and consistently hopeless. No one even brings me to Christmas mass any more because as soon as I get in the doors I become this twittering idiot.

"Religious rash! Help!"

I've even been kicked out of Wiccan circles in the dead of winter for making fun of the ceremonial dagger/steak knife. This would not be a noteworthy problem if it weren't also for the fact that almost every person I've ever fallen in love with did not have an extreme sense of religious purpose.

I could be eating pizza in the deepest depths of hell and fall for a vegan Jehovah's Witness. It never fails. It is because of this that, despite my lack of faith, I've almost become a Buddhist, a Witch, and even a Mormon (though that's a VERY complicated and long story). I've never managed to be any of those things for very long mind you... which explains why I'm so often single.

Having said that, the scariest thing I almost ever became (a born-again Christian) had nothing to do with love (which is a relief because I think in that case I would have been in really big trouble). That, actually, is a long and involved story that has a little to do with skiing, a little to do with a best friend's betrayal, and something to do with the Godliness of George Michael.

My best friend in grade nine was a tall and sickly creature named Katie B, a born-again Christian whose only beef with God (who was otherwise AMAZING) was that he had given her a crown of blond ringlets that were toasting and straightening with age. Katie said she liked me because I bore my own brown locks with what she thought was a suitable mix of humility and acceptance. I actually liked my hair and so was not so impressed by this statement. The only problem with our friendship, aside from the fact that I found Katie to be somewhat insulting at times, was that Katie thought I was going to hell because, unlike her, I didn't believe in God.

I stopped believing in God when I was six and my father told me that the tooth fairy, the Easter Bunny, and Santa Claus were, for all intents and purposes, him. (Technically I should have suspected this a long time ago, like around the time that the tooth fairy started leaving me I.O.U. notes on my father's stationery instead of quarters.)

The discovery of this hoax had a profound impact on my opinion of faith. I found it difficult to believe that my parents would expect me to believe in Jesus and the Holy Trinity when clearly, for a large part of my life, they had been lying to me about everything else.

"So let me get this straight. There's no Easter Bunny, but on the third day, He rose from the dead?"

I was not persuaded by the bible or the many Jesus movies I was shown. In fact, this dissuaded me even further from believing in God and his family, since the majority of the movies and books I had read were also lies. Even the Pope, whom I had gone to see when he drove to Toronto in his Popemobile, did little to change my opinion of this religious charade. Certainly he was a charismatic man who had his own parade. But didn't thousands gather every year to wave at a man who was pretending to be Santa Claus? Explain that!

Kate, who was of stronger, Christian stock, saw my ramblings on God for what they were: a feeble excuse for my lack of devotion to Jesus Christ. And though even she participated when I pulled out my tarot cards at Sophie Johnson's birthday, a secret God-fearing plan must have been secretly brewing in the back of her mind.

The opportunity for my conversion presented itself several months later when Katie's bible group organized a ski trip to Lake Placid over March break. Technically, as both a non-Christian and a skier of questionable skill (I have this theory that few Japanese Canadians are really good skiers but that may not be true), there was no reason for me to go on this trip. I probably wouldn't have if it hadn't been for one crucial deciding factor: BOYS. It pains me to know that my libido was the instrument of my demise, but really, I was a mindless bimbo back then. I was fifteen years old with lips still stinging from a sustained stubbly face sucking with an anonymous boy who came to a school dance. My body ached for experience and I allowed my loins to take over when social decisions were being made.

You go to an all-girls' private school, my loins reasoned, and turning down a chance to mingle with boys when you go to a private school is like admitting to your mother that you were late for dinner because you were masturbating in your room. But born-again Christians? *Born-again my ass,* my body noted, dreaming of nights huddled against the cold of the snow. I handed in my $200 and sign-up sheet.

I should have backed out. I should have backed out when Katie's parents called our house to congratulate me for making this decision. I absolutely should have backed out when our bus pulled up with a big THREE CHEERS FOR JESUS banner on the side.

Believe me, if it had been possible to dump my body out the side of the bus when the first round of "He's got the whole world in his hands" started up, I would have. Suddenly, with my hand pressing on the cold glass of the impossibly fast-moving bus, it occurred to me that the only person I would have any chance to press myself up against that week was Jesus.

The only other person who appeared to show me any signs of interest was Stephan, the 6'3" lumberjack-like bible leader who had clapped my back when I boarded the bus and had hollered: "Oh I sense some possibility here!" And… like… I'm sure he didn't mean THAT kind of possibility.

I saw a movie once in grade seven about how cults pull people off the street and make them watch endless movies about Sun Yung Moon until they finally submit to the beauty of his shiny forehead. My religious studies teacher told me you can tell you're being courted by a cult by what they feed you. *Sugary foods and carbohydrates,* she told us, *sure signs of a cult.* Beware the Hare Krishnas who meet you at airports in gold and red sheets, smacking their tambourines to that funky rhythm to which we are all so susceptible (especially when we've just got off a plane with all its tiny realities, little salt and peppers, little coffees). Behind that gentle rhythm is a band full of men ready to lure you back to their lair to shove you full of Mars bars and lies. Turns out that it's the Christians filling us with bread and wine, not the Krishnas (who are more inclined to make sure their potential followers have a healthy vegetarian diet).

Two days into my skiing adventure, I was spinning in a brine of Christianity, corn chips, and Pepsi. They were the only things I could ever find to eat and drink that hadn't been boiled or fried beyond recognition. Though during the day I was free to ski with my new God-fearing friends, at night I was secluded in a room with the two other non-Christians suckered into skiing with Jesus. Stephan, who was still clapping me on the back, each time with more force, made us sit in a circle and listen to George Michael's album "Listen without Prejudice." I found this a little insulting, as our CD Walkmans had recently been confiscated because we were all listening to filth.

It turns out that there's a lot of deep religious significance in George Michael's lyrics. This is ironic when you consider that he must have written a lot of them in the throes of what we now know to be closeted homosexual ecstasy. Not that any of us knew that at the time. Lying on the floor of a dark room, we listened to the song "Praying for Time" over and over again. I could hear the sounds of my fellow atheists breathing as I plotted ways to seek my revenge on Katie, whom I had not seen since I boarded the bus to Hades. At the end of the night we were given a sheet to take to bed.

These are the days of the open hand

They will not be the last

Look around now

These are the days of the beggars and the choosers

Q: WHO DO YOU THINK THE BEGGARS AND CHOOSERS ARE?

This is the year of the hungry man

Whose place is in the past

Hand in hand with ignorance

And legitimate excuses

Q: ARE THERE LEGITIMATE EXCUSES?

Surely if there was ever a time for desperate measures,
this was it. Positive that my parents would understand
my atheist plight, I placed a last-minute desperate call to
them, but no one was home. That night I found out that
Kate had been caught necking with some boy in his bunk
and was kicked out of the camp.

But we'll take our chances

Because God's stopped keeping score

I guess somewhere along the way

He must have let us all out to play

Turned his back and all God's children

Crept out the back door

Q: HAVE YOU EVER FELT ALONE?

Yes!!!

The second-to-last day, at the height of my misery, Stephan met me at the entrance to the ski resort. "You and me," he said, smiling a big white Christian smile, "are going to conquer these here slopes. Okay?"

"Sure."

As we walked, Stephan hummed the George Michael song "Freedom."

"Do you realize," he said, as we waited for our ski lift chair to scoop us up, "that all your woes can be cured by Jesus? That with Jesus you'll never be alone, never be afraid again?"

His face squished between goggles and toque two sizes too small, Stephan leaned forward and gave me what was likely intended to be a comforting smile. Below my feet a mile of emptiness separated me from the steep decline below. I was trapped.

"The world is a troubling place when you have no faith to stand on. When you have Jesus at your side, you're always standing on something."

At that moment, as if on cue, the ski lift began to rock back and forth in the wind. My feet felt tugged down by my heavy skis as my ass slipped sideways into what I was just now realizing was an incredibly flimsy metal frame. Stephan smiled and pushed his face into the breeze like a Labrador puppy sticking its head out of the car window.

It suddenly occurred to me that if he were right, Stephan

had absolutely nothing to fear. If we were to plummet hundreds of feet to the ground below, he would go to meet his maker. I, recently abandoned by my stinky friends, starving and scared, would be going to hell. I made a bold and uncalculated decision.

"Okay," I said, "I believe."

"Do you accept Jesus Christ as your Lord and Saviour?" He had the bluest eyes, as blue as the sky in a Jesus postcard.

"Yes."

I've wondered, since then, what Stephan thought made me decide to convert at that moment. I watched a documentary once on David Berg, founder of the Children of God and inventor of the infamous "Flirty Fishing," a kind of sexy moniker for religious recruiting. I wonder now if he thought I was eventually won over by his good looks and grasp of George Michael lyrics. I can't tell you for sure what it was. I'm fairly sure it wasn't his grasp of George Michael.

As soon as the words passed my chapped lips I regretted them. I felt like some sort of folk hero giving up his armour to an evil wizard. Stephan let out a series of bellowing laughs, punching me playfully on the arm as we prepared to ski down the slope, presumably to spread the word of my recent conversion.

I shot down the hill like a bat out of hell, my mind racing with the consequences of my actions. The thing is this: it was one thing entirely to not believe in God, it was quite another to *lie* and say I did. Despite what George Michael might believe, I felt sure that God could respect a non-believer more than He could a hypocrite. Behind me Stephan zig-zagged down the hill, confident in his victory, waving his poles at me as he took sharp corners.

Watching him struggle with the little straps on his poles (which you're really not supposed to loop around your wrists), I heard a quiet, clear little voice in the back of my mind. "Not only have you just accepted Jesus Christ as your Saviour," it said, "but this dork is going to take credit for YOUR soul."

"Stephan," I whispered, as we did our ski boot robot walk into the lodge.

"What?"

"I take it back."

I had been a born-again Christian for all of four minutes.

"You what?!"

At first I was worried that there would be no takesies/backsies for this particular bargain. Fortunately I had signed no papers. My soul was doomed but intact. Stephan shook his head.

"You must be a very sad little girl," he said, "to lie to me like that."

I wanted to punch him in the shoulder and assure him that I was still full of possibilities but didn't. That night, for reasons of my own, I slept in the back of the bus, eager to return to my religion — and George Michael-free home.

That week I found out that Katie got mono from the boy she'd kissed, who lived in Etobicoke and wasn't returning her calls. It made me feel a little good hearing that: evil and non-Christian, but good nonetheless.

Cats Are Not People:

Questions you should ask yourself when considering the
line (and how you cross it) between cats and people

A LOT OF PEOPLE are going to get mad when they see
that I've written this. Really I don't think I've written anything bad (maybe I'm a little harsh at points). I'm just
saying there's a line. Cats have feelings, they're living sen-
tient beings, but they're not people; there's a difference. I
shouldn't even have to explain it. Anyway, this is just a short
list of questions I think cat owners should ask themselves. Are you crossing the line between pet and person?

1 Who eats first in your house, you or the cat? It's the cat,
isn't it?

Maybe I'm mean, but in my house, humans eat first. It's a food-chain thing, in my opinion, plus I read somewhere that feeding animals first gives them a warped vision of where they stand in the family (i.e., it gives them the impression that they're heads of the pack). A lot of people I know are always giving their cats that "little extra" because they look hungry. A little hint: cats always look hungry, it's the eye-shape, trust me.

2 How long do you hold the door open when you let the cat out?

When you open the door and let your cat out, a minute is about all a cat should really get to decide whether or not he/she wants out. Holding the door for any more than a minute looks and is stupid and lets all the cold air in; plus it's useless. I mean, really, what does a cat have to decide, it's not like your cat has any major appointments that he/she *has* to go to, so that keeping them in would be a big deal. And it's not as if your cat is stalling inside the house for any particularly useful reason, like he/she's worried she forgot something (hmmm, where's my purse?). Cats either go outside or they stay in, period.

3 Tell me you don't dress your cat up in little outfits.

There is *really* nothing more embarrassing than people who put clothes on their pets. If someone set up a bill to make that sort of thing illegal, I would sign it. Putting clothes on pets is a sign of the owner's insanity and a pet's shame. Clothes are for people, not pets. I can't stress that enough. (The only exception that I can think of is those little things you put on dogs' paws when you take them for walks in the snow. Okay, those things are acceptable. Nothing else though.) There's no way you're going to get a dress or sweater on a cat without an intense struggle. Count that as a sign. Collars, a necessity for identification, are one thing, but when buying a collar an owner should recall that a collar is not something a cat can see (because it's on their neck), so kitty approval, or kitty consideration, is not necessary. Anyone who spends any more than five dollars on a collar should reconsider their priorities.

4 Do you talk to your cat? Okay, nothing wrong with that. Do you expect your cat to respond?

There's got to be somewhere to draw the line between talking to your pet and considering your cat's feelings when you talk. Cats, I think, as a rule, don't speak English (or even French), and so while I'm sure they're willing to humour us humans when we babble on, I don't think they take anything we say personally or to heart. Generally I think cats think humans make very little sense and so I doubt they're even paying attention to much that we say, unless it's something along the lines of food or dinner. I had this girlfriend once who would get severely pissed when I said anything bad about her cat. Oh, I'm sorry, should I remove myself from the room, should I whisper, talk in abstracts? On a personal note, I'm sure my cat,

Stanley, thinks his name is "HEY!" which is what I yell at him when he's standing on something he's not supposed to be on.

5 Do you think your cat is mean to you?

The life of a cat owner is not without its little ups and downs. Ever come home to a shredded couch or a room of scattered papers? Cats do fucked-up things; it's in their nature. The important thing is not to take these things personally. Sometimes a ripped-up chair, especially with cats (I'm not sure if this applies to dogs), is just a ripped-up chair. Cat owners have this tendency to become super guilt-ridden moms at the sign of any destruction. It really must stop. The only thing you really have to worry about is cat barf. Cat barf, especially on your pillow or bed, is usually a sign of some pretty intense feelings or an infection of some sort and should be seen to ASAP. The same goes with urine. Cat pee, outside the box, is pretty serious and it's okay to freak out and worry.

Just remember, moms and dads, it's okay to love, worship, and adore your pet. It is, in fact, advisable to love your pet. But sanity is golden in this day and age. Learn to draw the line. It will make you and your pet happier entities.

The Great Communicators

for Zoe

FAMILY

I come from a long line of women who slam doors. On my mother's side are three generations of women who "spoke softly," all the while saying things like, "What do you think *you* did wrong?" and "Oh no, no, no, I'm *fine*, why wouldn't I be fine?"

"Well?"

My mother's side of the family speaks loudest with the little words that don't even make it across the tight lines of their little lips (not to criticize, of course, since they're my little lips too). When I relax my face, maternal genetics kick in and a little dissatisfied frown pinches my mouth, a familial look of reserved judgement and vague disapproval… like there's a bad smell in the air and it's not me.

So it must be you.

At parties people approach me and ask, "Are you mad?"

"No," I say, "this is how I look when I'm relaxed."

The only solution I've found is to talk, keeping my mouth in constant motion so it won't settle into that little frown.

There is a proud tradition of silence on the paternal side of my family; there is the option not to slam the door but to quietly, subtly, raise an eyebrow when a door is slammed. The men in my family are not big talkers, not even really fans of big talkers… big talkers like me.

My father and I have had a particular and consistent relationship when it comes to communication: I have a lot to say, and he doesn't want to hear it.

My father does not remember my first words. Every time I ask him what my first word was, he gives me a different answer.

Two years ago it was "Daddy."

Last week, out of curiosity, I asked him again and he said, "Coffee."

"Coffee?"

"Uhhhhh… Golf."

I can only guess that the occasion of my first words is lost on my father because I have had so much to say since then.

My father has scars on his legs from where my little five year old nails dug into his ankle as he dragged me across the floor screaming, "I have a *story*! I have a story to *tell* you."

"I don't want to *hear* your story," he would yell, limping into his study. "Go away."

For this and other reasons, the most time my father will ever spend with me is over a game of Scrabble. I am extremely competitive when it comes to Scrabble. I am my most quiet when faced with a set of seven tiles imprinted with a valued letter system. Having accepted the grim reality that I cannot play Monopoly, or any sport involving being outside, or inside, or in water, I approach this game as a lifeboat of potential victory. There's a theory floating around that as a writer, I should be a pretty good Scrabble player.

Advantage: Me.

Words are supposed to be my trade. Unfortunately Scrabble is not a game for wordsmiths or even word lovers. Scrabble is a game for mathematicians and accountants. More a love of strategy than a love of diction.

Advantage: Dad.

My dad says I lose because I save up for big words, which is his way of saying that I like to show off. Like the fact that I'll forgo putting down "IRON" to save up for "IRONY" is a suggestion of stupidity, rather than, say, intelligence.

Last Christmas, during a particularly brutal third-round game, my dad told me I should stop worrying about using big words and start worrying about *how* I use big words, which, ironically, is the best advice he's ever given me.

PSYCHIATRISTS

Every psychiatrist I've ever met has had a different method of getting me to communicate; some, obviously, better than others. I once went to a psychiatrist whose office was a tickle trunk full of crayons, magazines, and dolls. The idea was to get you wrapped up in your environment with the hope that eventually you would share your feelings as you searched for a decent outfit for Ken. I used to get into fights about whether or not I was allowed to bring home my drawings and my newly dressed Ken dolls. My shrink said I had difficulty discerning the feasibility of my demands.

Him: YOU WANT TOO MUCH.

Me: You think so?

When I finally left him, I stole a pair of sparkly Ken doll pants. I figured it was just deserts since I clearly wasn't cured, even after six months of drawing daisies on construction paper and talking about my mother.

The last psychiatrist wanted me to lie down on a couch so I could "free associate." It was supposed to help me concentrate on myself instead of staring at this shrink. I worried though, about this particular tactic, because: 1) if I wanted to just lie down and free associate I could do that at home with the voices in my head and 2) I had had one or two incidents where I'd been free associating and I'd heard distinct little snoring noises.

There's nothing like having to stop your diatribe about why women aren't trustworthy to sneak a peek to see if your shrink is awake. I left her too, not because she wasn't awake, but because she denied falling asleep. When I confronted her about it, she suggested I had trust issues. I did. That and it was getting harder and harder to talk to this woman. She had a whole list of words I wasn't allowed to say. Like "hate" or "angry." Instead I had to use phrases like "makes me uncomfortable" and "arouses feelings of rejection." I found these phrases inadequate. I learned to hate them. They made me angry.

Eventually, one afternoon, I tiptoed out while she slept. I left a Post-it on her forehead that said: Now THIS makes me uncomfortable.

THE LOVERS

Lovers are supposed to have a kind of implicit line of communication. My roommate firmly believes that a common attraction opens up a link between two people through which unspoken messages can be transmitted.

Presumably messages like:

"I want to sleep with you."

"Me too."

Céline Dion, who saves her voice between shows (or at least she did before she retired to have a baby), has a special code she taps on the phone receiver. One tap means yes and two taps mean no. Aside from that, she has a whole slew of secret codes that only she and her husband, Rene, know.

Tap tap tap, tap tap tap = I know you're old enough to be my father but I love you anyway.

When I was in university I lived down the hall from a yuppie gay couple, Todd and Jon, who spoke their own language, *ToddyJon*. It was a gobbledygook speak, pre-syllabic, and embarrassing. The kind of stuff your mom says to you when she licks a Kleenex and uses it to wash your face. I could hear them whispering it in the laundry room, giggling as they came up the stairs, each holding a handle of their trusty IKEA laundry basket. In their language, Jon explained, there was no word for *fight* or *angry*. Instead they had a million different words for *tacky*, six different words for *yummy*.

I was pretty bitter about it at the time, jealous, probably, because my then-girlfriend and I didn't have a secret language, only a lot of poetry, which we seemed to be writing more out of a selfish artistic need than any desire to communicate with each other.

"We have common *references*," she told me, "isn't that enough?" At the time I thought allusions were a poor substitute for a secret word for kiss.

Todd and Jon lived together for three years, until Jon died of cancer. I never got to ask if there was ever any word in their language for death. Maybe they would simply substitute their word for "good-bye," which is sadly too cooey and strange to communicate on paper.

I wondered afterwards if Todd was ever lonely knowing he would never have someone to speak to in that language again.

My then ex-girlfriend wrote a piece about them for the funeral, three years before I got around to it. I'm a little bitter about that too.

WRITERS

Today I live with writers, a community of men and women who'd rather write it than say it, who can create beautiful stories on paper and yet are unable to talk to people at parties or even answer the phone. This is often confusing for people who call us or invite us to parties. Many end up feeling a little snubbed by our silence. The thing is that what you write is a much easier catastrophe to manage than what you say. You can move words around, erase and rewrite them ad nauseum. Something spoken, of course, can never be unspoken, erased, or undone. Even something as stupid as, "Def Leppard is a BAND? Really?"

Writers, especially writers who are not up to par on their rock trivia, have to be careful with words, which are dangerous things and are easily misinterpreted.

Which reminds me of a little story.

When I was fifteen years old my favourite band in the world was R.E.M. and my favourite song in the world was "Losing My Religion." I loved that song. I embraced it with the fortitude and drive of a depressed teenager. I made it my anthem and angrily guarded it and its meaning from behind my black pointy goth bangs. I loathed the fact that jock boys and cheerleaders also loved that song and put it on their mix tapes. I was sure they couldn't possibly comprehend that song the way I did, understanding what it was like to actually lose your religion, your faith, your understanding of the very principles that the universe rotated around.

Shortly after that, I turned seventeen and started loving the equally painful and angsty "Killing in the Name" by Rage Against the Machine. The jock boys loved that song too, but there was the added bonus of being able to spike them with your jewellery when you danced to the song in the mosh pit, belting out the words. The point of this story as it relates to the subject of communication comes ten years later when I watched a Live-by-Request special with R.E.M. On it Michael Stipe talked about the phrase "losing my religion," which, it turns out, isn't about religion at all. It's about talking to someone you're falling for, when the conversation gets away from you and you end up giving away a part of yourself that you weren't expecting to; and it feels like you're losing your religion.

I like that better than my goth interpretation. It makes me wonder if Michael Stipe ever answers his phone, or goes to parties.

ME

Every once in a while I get this nagging worry that I might some day run out of words... things to say and things to write. I have dreams where I have to write long letters using fridge-magnet poetry, and I can't find any "the" tiles. I wake up screaming.

I think of two things when this happens. The first thing I think of is my friend Susie, who every year (right about the time Seasonal Affective Disorder is affecting the Greater Toronto Area) gets a wicked case of writer's block and renews her theory that there are perhaps only so many stories out there to be written. This theory is based on a segment she heard once on the radio about some scientist who had calculated that given the existing number of musical notes, by the year 2003 the world will be out of songs. This theory typically sends Susie into a tailspin of darkness, keeping her in her apartment for weeks, lying on a sofa, watching A&E, until February.

Of course some time around February Susie always thinks of something incredible to write, so maybe I shouldn't worry, I think. Maybe it will be all right. There must always be something to say, mustn't there, even if it's the wrong thing. Even if it means picking up the phone and losing a bit of your religion.

The second thing I think, every time this happens, always puts a smile on my face. Whenever I'm at a loss for words I think: won't my father be pleased?

These Are the Rules

for Abi

1 There is no such thing as clash or mismatch but there is such a thing as ugly. And nothing goes with ugly.

2 Shoes make the world go round. A good pair of shoes will make you a better person. (I know it's hard to believe but it's true.)

3 There is no excuse for Converse shoes. See above.

4 There is no such thing as too cheap but be advised that there are some polyester hybrids known to cause considerable skin irritation: something to consider before you buy those hot-pant undies from a booth on Spadina.

5 T-shirts with cartoon characters are not a) cute or b) funny; they are c) yucky and suggestive of your IQ level.

6 The only people on this planet allowed to combine nylons and Nikes are secretaries. Secretaries don't like doing it, neither should you.

7 Burn the banana clip. The minute it showed up on *Star Trek* as a prop it ceased to be allowable for anyone to wear one on his/her head.

8 White socks may be cheap and available but they glow in the dark when you're in dance clubs with black lighting. Michael Jackson got away with this in "Thriller" but look at him now.

9 Never have hair that is smarter than the city you live in.

A couple of months ago I made a hairstyle change based on a dream I had. In my dream I was visiting with the president (of the United States) to discuss the impending Lewinsky crisis, and I had this fabulous hair. I kept looking at it in the mirror, unable to concentrate on what the president was saying.

"Wow," I kept thinking, "I look amazing. And, I'm in the Oval Office."

I woke up and made a sketch right away. That Friday, I handed the sketch over to my hairdresser Jakes.

"Make me look like this," I said.

Jakes said it was the first time that someone handed over a sketch from a dream. Usually, he said, it's a head shot of either Princess Diana or Jennifer Aniston.

I personally think it's really sad to cop style from a TV show — but I do it all the time.

What was special about this particular hairstyle was the colour. I wanted a big black-blue mushroom bob and hot-pink bangs.

"Like a My Little Pony," I told Jakes as he lowered me into the sink, "only more sophisticated."

"Sure thing toots." Jakes was the only person who was allowed to call me toots, and that was only because he was otherwise very obedient.

He did my hair so I looked exactly like I did in my dream. I was ten minutes late for everything I had to do that day because I spent the whole day staring at my reflection in the windows on the street. Now that is the sign of a good haircut.

Apparently I was not the only one captivated with my new 'do. On the first day alone, perhaps on the day my bangs were at their shiniest, eight people stopped to comment on my bangs. Mostly the comments were little more than, "HEY YOU!"

Some people put a little thought into it. "You know what you look like," the lady at my local Dominion told me, "one of those Teletubby things."

"That's stupid," I retorted. "I don't look anything like a Teletubby thing, I look like a My Little Pony."

This was my first inkling that I might be living in a city of uncool idiots.

After about a week I started to lose my patience. It wasn't just that people seemed to enjoy my hair (hey, I'm a performer, enjoy all you want), it was the perplexity and puzzlement. And the overwhelming desire for directions.

I knew things had got out of hand when the driver of the cab I was riding in stopped his car with the meter running and actually turned around to ask, "Hey, how did you do that to your hair?"

I nearly exploded. "Am I paying for this?!" I screamed.

This hair was starting to cost me money.

At first I was fairly accommodating, explaining to those who asked that my shining 'do was the result of a combination of peroxide (lots and lots of peroxide) and a pink dye called "Fudge." By the end of the month I had lost any grip I might ever have had on social generosity and my answers became increasingly trite. I think the last time someone asked me about my pink bangs I retorted calmly, "Last week I slipped on the rug and hit my head and it's been like this ever since."

"You know," my friend Jessica said, "style is something you must often pay for in more ways than one."

Hmmm.

But of course the final straw was when my boss, my THEN-boss, who was a Toronto arts sophisticate selling overly expensive paintings to housewives in Forest Hill, pulled me into a meeting to show me off to her clients.

"She's just like a Spice Girl," one of the Gucci ladies said.

"I'm not a Spice Girl," I sneered, "I'm a Ricki Lake guest. Everybody knows that."

This was shortly before I lost that job and dyed my hair back to its not-so-natural-but-close-enough-to-blue-black, which I sport to this day.

"You'll lose your cool," my friends moaned when I told them the news as I sat basting in L'Oréal Midnight Blue. "Beware normalcy."

Needless to say I was less than amused by my friends' rather *un*-suave support-system methods and pushed on... because hey man, there's something to be said for being able to walk down the street without being accosted by every Torontonian out and about who has never heard of hair dye outside the colour scheme of brown, black, red, and blond.

And hey man, let's face it, there's something to be said for THE RULES. THE RULES, as listed above, are there for a reason.

This is not to say that each and every one of us should not strive in our every action and purchase to achieve the maximum amount of cool we can muster. I'm just saying there are rules. There is ugly and there is cool. There's velvet and there's velour, and sadly, there exists a large population in Toronto that does not know the difference between a My Little Pony and a Teletubby.

Call me if you ever get confused.

Sometimes Psychics Let You Down

*

LET ME MAKE it clear before I proceed that I am the first person to mock those who dabble in the unknown, the mystic, and anything else faintly smelling of incense. I have never had any mercy for the weak and I admit to enjoying a joke at their expense. It is for this reason that I informed few people of the recent $90 charge on my phone bill credited to the infamous Psychic Alliance.

I can only say that I was, at the time, in an extremely fragile state of mind. Allow me to explain. For as long as I can remember, I have always been... a little nutty.

Specifically, there is nothing in this world that scares me more than travel. The result of the combination of travel and me is a huge ball of stress. Add to this a fear of flying, and you have the essence of me: a little nutty.

It is no surprise then that I reacted the way I did two months ago when my employers told me they were sending me to Los Angeles. The average person would react with glee; I went on what you might call a paranoia spree. On the night before my flight I downed five litres of Coca-Cola (The Official Drink of Nervous-Disorder Patients) and a pizza pie built for four. Panic feeding. Think Brian Wilson. I had that generic nervous-break-down look you see on students during exams. It was my first flight in over two years... from one side of the continent to the other. Think of that: one side of the continent to the other in five hours. Can't be natural. Sounds too good to be true. Think Titanic. That morning I had had lunch with the only woman in Toronto more paranoid than I was.

"Gee," she'd said, "you don't think with the whole Kosovo war going on that there might be any plane bombings would you? I mean, that's the reason I won't fly."

(Me, going completely white.)

"No, of course there won't be any bombings."

(AHHHHH!)

Now, nearing 12:00 p.m., I was avoiding the news war coverage like the plague and sucking down whole cupcakes like a demon vacuum. At some point, in mid-cupcake, I caught a glimpse of a commercial for the infamous Psychic Alliance.

Do you believe in fate?

"Hey! You! Stressed about work? Looking for love? Nervous about the future?"

Nervous about TRAVEL?

"Call us at the Psychic Alliance. Put your mind at ease."

Not since the night I got home from losing my virginity and went to call my best friend have I ever dialled a number that fast.

"Hi there, this is Danielle speaking, I'll be your psychic this evening. What's your name, honey?"

"Mariko."

"Can you tell me when your birthday is?"

"December 22, 1975."

"Oh, on the cusp. You're very complex. How can I help you?"

There must be some sort of chemical effect that takes place when someone says you're complex. (Possibly this is because we harbour a secret fear that we're boring.) In any case, listening to that deep voice, I instantly plunged into a dark pool of blind faith.

Ignorance is expensive bliss.

"Ah, Mariko," Danielle cooed reassuringly, " I'm getting some very strong vibes here. This is your first call, isn't it?"

"Oh my God, how did you know that?"

"I'm psychic, honey."

(They also ask you that before they connect you.)

I made up my mind that if Danielle gave me even the slightest hint of a negative vibe I would cancel my flight and hole up in my apartment until she told me it was safe to go out again.

Danielle told me to wait while she consulted my cards.

"Well," she finally said triumphantly, "I can see your problem right here. The Lovers. You think your boyfriend is cheating on you."

"I beg your pardon."

Danielle halted, faint sounds of shuffling in the background.

"I also see some financial concerns here... that cheque you just got is going to bounce."

"What?"

Danielle paused again. Judging her next move carefully.

"Why don't you tell me what question you want answered?"

Wrong!

"What do you mean *tell you*," I hollered, "*you're* the psychic. *You* are supposed to answer my questions! Haven't you seen the commercial?"

Danielle guessed again. "Is your problem job related?"

There's nothing like sitting on the phone with a tele-phone psychic and realizing you're an idiot... an idiot who's paying fifteen dollars an hour to talk to another idiot, who thinks you're an idiot.

I couldn't even think of a good insult to hurl at Danielle. I hung up in disgust (mostly with myself).

The next day I slept through my alarm and almost missed my airport limo. I spent an enraged ten minutes at Customs looking for my passport. I had carelessly wedged it in a novel I was reading and forgotten about it. I ended up on the plane squished between an anxious teenage boy and a born-again Christian named Helen. She was wearing a shirt that said: SINNERS BEWARE.

Well, I thought, at least if I crash I'm taking these two with me. About an hour later, during turbulence, I had an intimate prayer session with Helen the born-again Christian.

I'm a religious Benedict Arnold. It's true.

Needless to say, despite or because of this character flaw, I made it through my trip unscarred.

As an end note, two weeks later I got a call from the bank telling me a cheque someone had written me had bounced.

I nearly passed out.

Hey, sometimes psychics let you down. Sometimes they don't.

Within Reason

*

My **FRIEND WENDY** has this theory that the reason she's not getting laid is because she's a Cancer with an Aries rising.

According to Walter, a telephone psychic to whom Wendy has paid a sum that cannot be spoken of, it's really not a good year for Cancers, especially Cancers with an Aries rising.

Wendy said when she told him when she was born he literally hissed through his teeth.

"Bad news honey."

For this and other reasons, this summer Wendy is going to board herself up in her condo with the big book of vegan cooking and a stack of textbooks to wait for things to start looking better. While Pluto and Venus get their act together, Wendy plans to learn as much about lentils, human psychology, and Brazil as humanly possible.

This is not the first time that someone whom I used to respect has suggested to me a reason that they're not getting laid that has something to do with "greater forces." I know one or two people who have a lingering suspicion that the reason they're not getting any has something to do with either God or the Goddess. I know one person who thinks it's because she can't decide between the Goddess and God (which I think is something you should decide anyway).

Though I suppose a lot of us could blame the greater cosmos for our problems, hoping to be part of the greater scheme of things, I can't help but feel that it's a little screwed up to blame one's lack of action on a freak alignment of the planets. I mean, I'm sure when the end comes it will be because of a big rock in outer space. Until then, you would think that big rocks have better things to do than fuck with our social lives.

There are a lot of far simpler and more obvious reasons that you could not be getting laid. I can personally think of at least eight, none of which have anything to do with rocks, karma, or God* (*as you understand Him/Her).

So in honour of my friend Wendy, who I never see any more, here is my list of possible reasons you're not getting any.

1

Your friends are too good-looking a.k.a. your friends are better looking than you.

There's something to be said for being the best-looking person you know. This isn't to say that you should seek out ugly people to hang out with, or that you should vocalize your knowledge that you are, in fact, the cutest banana in the bunch. But you might just want to look into levelling the playing field a little by not befriending a bunch of really attractive people. There's nothing worse for your libido than having the reputation of being someone who is the friend of a really good-looking person. This also applies to really funny people. And really slutty people. There are two sluts and a comedian whose phone calls I'm avoiding right now and I feel better for it.

2

You live in a backward city with too many hang-ups.

I'm not saying that people outside large urban centres will always have trouble dating, but there's something to be said for supply and demand. The nice thing about cities is that with so many people milling around out there, you have a good chance of meeting someone who's the kind of weird you're into, who's also into... openly into, your kind of weird. It's all about the law of averages. I have a friend who thinks it's possible to move anywhere now because the Internet, in her words, "connects us all." I got a similar line from an anonymous Alaskan Dyke Yahoo chatter, DykeAlaska222, a couple months ago. The Internet may connect us all but it's not, in my opinion, going to use its "magic mouse" to reach out and touch us any time soon, especially when that mouse is in Alaska. So until then, stay close to urban centres that house the people that will (touch you that is). And stay away from AlaskaDyke222, who I suspect is a teenage boy who got his hands on a copy of *On Our Backs*.

3 It's winter (it's too cold).

One of the hardest places to get laid, in my experience, is Montreal in February, not because there aren't a lot of good-looking people there but because it's too damn cold. Aside from the fact that everyone's sick from January on, it's extremely difficult to advertise your availability inside a sixteen-pound parka with a huge wool scarf wrapped around your face. You could be sexy and smiling and it's so cold no one cares. I will say that Montreal is really fun right around September because everyone's scrambling to cozy up to someone before the ever-so-attractive Seasonal Affective Disorder hits. Every October in Montreal is like the last five minutes on the Titanic, only French and less expensive. (Incidentally I used to feel really bad about the whole SAD Montreal until I was talking to a friend who lived there and she said, "Well God, at least we don't have to work a full work week to pay rent." And after that I didn't feel so bad.)

4
Everyone thinks you're sleeping with your best friend.

There's nothing wrong with friends, but in a world rampant with miscommunication and mixed messages, it's worth paying a little attention to appearances. If you are a) a single woman whose best friend is b) a single woman and you are both c) always going out together and leaving together and spending all your time on the phone, it is not terribly unlikely that people would start to think you are d) seeing each other. If this has never crossed your mind as a possibility you e) are incredibly naïve and/or f) should possibly consider the possibility that you should sleep together. Alternatively you could assert your availability by randomly making out with different people when you go out together… your call.

5
You're a fag hag.

Fags are incredible people and we should all make an effort to spend as much time as possible with them but there is no breed of woman more single than hardcore fag hags. Fags have absolutely nothing to offer women sexually, except maybe a little bit of potentially merited and yet sometimes overly harsh criticism. Other than that, they will not fix you up, they will not take you to places where you can hookup, and they're usually so consumed with their own problems getting booty they couldn't give a shit whether or not you're getting yours (even if they really like you they could give a shit). If you're going to be a fag hag you'd better get a booty connection set up first because otherwise you might as well be an agoraphobic in the deep of a Montreal winter.

6 You're a comedian.

Okay, technically this is not yet a reason for not getting laid, but I have this theory that comedians like myself and other nameless people are due for a severe dry spell because we are always using our sexual experiences as material. I know one comedian who gets threats now every time she sleeps with someone because no one wants to end up in her routine. One day I'm going to start writing some historical novels and when I do, you all will know it was because someone I was dating finally laid down the law (until then it's a free-for-all).

7 You're a terrible dancer.

I'm not exactly sure if being a bad dancer is a reason for not getting laid, but it does seem notable that good dancers are always getting laid. It's a little bit of reverse logic, I mean, if good dancing is sexy and alluring, then bad dancing is likely to be something of a turn-off. Plus if you're doing that dance where you spiral your arms in wild and unpredictable circles it's possible no one is sleeping with you because no one can get near you without getting a hand in the face. If you think you are a good dancer and you're not getting laid, you should consider the possibility that you are not a good dancer. Speaking of which...

8 You're a bad kisser.

If you're bringing a lot of people home and kissing them and then not getting laid (which is kind of like not getting laid but a little worse), then it's time to consider the possibility that you're a bad kisser. If in doubt, ask if you can kiss one of your friends and get them to give you their abject opinion. The general rule for kissing, in my opinion, is that less is more. You can always add something on to a kiss as you go along, but taking stuff away is like trying to take back something you said. Once it's out there that you have a thing for licking the underside of someone's nose, it's out there. I think it's a good idea to stay away from the nose period for the first little while, possibly because I once went home with this woman who started to lick and bite my nose and I was really horny but I went home because, frankly, that is really gross.

I shared this list with my friend La Rue and she agreed with me on all points except the "cold" one. La Rue said people in Iceland are renowned for being demons in the sack and they have no trouble getting laid.

Possible reason to travel to Iceland.

After further consideration, she added that there really isn't anything wrong with not getting laid, the only thing any of us should worry about, she said, is the possibility that we aren't getting laid because we're assholes.

If only because we should all make an effort not to be assholes, regardless of whether or not we're getting laid.

Angry Naked Women

*

DID YOU EVER have one of those days when you look like shit and you feel like shit and then someone gives you like a *minute* dosage of attitude and you think, "Well, it should just be legal to kill this person?"

Okay, well that's what this is about.

To all the little-butted, skinny people in the audience, I apologize in advance. All I can say is that you should all just be grateful that I'm here today and beyond that, you should be thankful that I didn't come here nude. Because let me tell you, as of late I am getting closer and closer to angry nakedness. The next time you see me I'll just be a pissed-off vagina. This past Wednesday at Toronto's Women's Bathhouse, when I looked around at all the naked bodies, what I saw was not an erotic display, but a practical option in a world where finding anything above a size twelve is like finding a virgin at a university dormitory.

I spent six hours yesterday scouring Toronto for a decent outfit that would fit over my thighs and I came to three conclusions:

1 This city sucks — it's hot, it contains no changing rooms bigger than my cat's litter box, and it's hot.

2 I hate all salespeople and blame them for the part they play in pushing a line of clothing that only fits a small fraction of the population (even if they aren't the ones who make the clothes, I blame them anyway).

3 All well-dressed fat people should be fucking worshipped and hailed as the gods they are.

Should I not choose to walk around for the rest of my days angry and nude, I'm going to opt instead to wear a T-shirt that says *I'm a well-dressed fat person and I deserve your respect for my efforts.*

And for those of you fed up with us fat chicks and our

bitching about our big fat asses and the problems they cause us, let me assure you no one is more tired of listening to me bitch about my big fat ass than me.

The only person who is possibly more wary of my big fat ass than me might be the retailer who tried to help me find an outfit amongst the racks at a store that shall remain nameless. Okay, it was the Gap. This poor man whose skinny ass I chewed into tiny bits after an hour of searching for something that would squeeze over my thighs… I swear, this poor man with all his efforts never had a chance of becoming anything more than a pothole in the road of my rage.

"You know," he said, as we neared the finale of my fitting routine, "maybe you should try a plus-size store."

I gathered my things, my courage, and my dignity, and pushed my way out of the tiny pen that had served as my dressing room.

"What's your name?" I asked.

"Ben," he said.

"Ben," I said. "Here's the situation Ben, I have to give this performance tomorrow and you know Ben, I was going to do a poem about my Visa card, but you know what I'm going to do now, Ben? I'm going to do a piece about snot-nosed Gap boys with little asses who work at boutiques that sell clothes for anorexic picks who make up all of 7% of the population."

"Don't you think that's just a little bitter," asked Ben.

"Do I look BITTER to you Ben," I asked, edging my sweaty body further and further into his personal space, "or do I look dangerously agitated?"

I left a sticker on the door that said:

WHEN THE REVOLUTION COMES, YOU AND YOUR
COHORTS WILL BE THE FIRST UP AGAINST THE WALL.

You think it's a joke, but I'm serious.

In the end, no thanks to Ben, I did find myself an outfit that day (a little polka-dotted number that makes me look immature but well-dressed), but memories of that particular exchange (and others like it) remain.

I have a plan.

I'll take my naked body to the streets in protest.

I'll pummel the public with what it insists on denying and avoiding: tons of mountainous, sexy flesh. I'll bare my boobs and squish my sweaty bum at strangers. I'll squeak against every available surface and leave strange marks to embarrass the public. I'll gather an army of fat angry naked soldiers and we'll take to the streets. We'll go to the Gap and touch all their clothes and use up all their perfume samples 'til they agree to stock sizes sixteen to thirty as standard practice.

We'll bring Toronto the Timid to its knees with the vengeance of our vaginas.

Look out, Ben, the revolution is coming.

Mark my words.

An Open Love Letter for the Homos

*

IT'S NO SECRET to those who know me that I am a big lover of homosexuals (homos). I absolutely adore homosexuals. I even like the word "homo," and if there weren't potential negative implications, I would have the word tattooed on my arm. Homo. It sounds like a Pop-Tart or something.

"Want a homo? It's got real fruit filling."

A lot of people think that the reason I love homosexuals is because I myself am gay. I seriously doubt this. There are a lot of people who are gay and don't even like homosexuals, including themselves. It's called QUEER LOATHING and there are a lot of movies about it. Chances are if you've ever seen a Queer movie, unless it was a dirty porno, it was a queer loathing movie. Maybe seven out of ten are. These are especially bad odds when you consider the fact that eight out of ten queer movies suck. Wonder why queers are always having sex? Maybe it's because all our movies are shitty. Why are there so many queer loathing movies? Who knows? Maybe if artists and film-makers were more together, less analytical, needy people, it wouldn't be such a problem.

So if being queer isn't the reason I like homos, what is?

Part of it has to do with sex. I'll let you in on a little secret here: I have never been more into sex than I am now. I'm even more into sex now than I was when I was HAVING sex all the time. I thank God I have the job I do, working at a sex-toy store. I swear, if it wasn't for the little army of sili-cone appendages I work with every day I think I would go absolutely MAD. Like M-A-D mad. This makes me wonder what priests do, no sex and absolutely nothing sexual to look at, just crosses and little boys and well… I guess we'd better not go there.

Gay people can totally relate to horniness. Being horny is a very gay thing to be; just like having lots of sex is a very gay thing to do. Homos have earned a tremendous amount of my respect for this. I think people who can readily admit that they are super fucking horny should be elected to office. At least then we'd know they weren't getting ready to go to war! A little bit of honesty can go a long way. On a broad tangent, I will add that this is why I'm not into nudists any more. I *used* to be, but then I saw a news program on nudists. They were so cute and roly-poly. Imagine a naked Patagonia ad, only sunburned and with pit hair. Halfway through the show the interviewer asked these two hairless guys if their nakedness had anything to do with sex and they said, *"No."* Can you believe it? They said it was a common misconception that nakedness leads to sex. Puhleeese. Okay, fine, maybe if you're eight, taking your shirt off and going for a swim is no biggie, but when you're fifty, playing volleyball with your dick swinging in the air? GET REAL.

So as I was saying, gay people, generally, have sex all the fucking time. They even have a parade about sex. It's called Gay Pride only "pride" is spelled F-U-C-K-M-E. For those of you who think that just because the mayor goes now that that changes anything, think again. Someone asked me once about the difference between homos and straights. I said all you have to do is look at the parades. Take the Rose Bowl: big parade. What do people do after it? Go home and watch football. Pride Day: big parade. What do people do during, before, and after it?

Well, what do you think they do? Go home and watch *The Wizard of Oz?*

There are exceptions, of course, such as Mardi Gras. For me, though, this is a booze thing. You can't tell me Mardi Gras ladies would still be all tittied up if they were sober. Pride, on the other hand, is naked and sexy with or without booze, despite the fact that nowadays, all the floats are sponsored by liquor companies.

The other notable distinction is the whole feeling around Pride, which is pretty positive, if steeped in the implication of plenteous, potentially meaningless sex. The whole atmosphere is set by the rainbow homo-pride flag. My theory is that in the beginning it was supposed to be a big PENIS, but then the lezzies got all mad and the size and type of penis came into question. Ask any homo though, what's at the end of that rainbow, and the answer is clear: SEX. You know that if heterosexuals one day decided to have a similar Heterosexual Pride parade, it would be absolutely disgusting. They would have to PAY people to get dressed up like sluts. Homos, on the other hand, will line up around the block to do it for FREE.

Where was I?

Aside from Pride Day, homos have a fairly decent gift for throwing parties. Heterosexuals know this and are therefore always copying homos when they party. How do I know this? Watched a beer commercial lately? Blatant homo-copying. It's like, no offence, but heterosexuals just DO NOT know how to party. Like, *really*. Having said that, the only thing worse than a het party, in my opinion, is a dyke party. The reason potlucks were invented was so dykes could alleviate some of the pain and suffering at their parties with food. And just so no one feels too superior, I should point out that the reason pot was originally invented was so that heterosexuals could blank out their parties, convincing themselves that whatever happened the night before was *fun*, rather than, say, mind-numbingly *booring*.

Don't even bother to deny any of this because I'm a dyke who used to be a straight girl, and I KNOW these things. I've thrown some of these parties. It's a stereotype, but it's a pretty fucking accurate one, so it's okay.

It always bothers me when people rag on stereotypes and the writers who use them. Like the other night I was eating with my parents and my mother was talking about this couple, this gay couple, both interior designers, and my father said something along the lines of "they must have a really nice house."

My mom got all mad, "YOU DON'T even KNOW them!" she said. "How can you say that? That's such a stereotype!"

A) They're interior designers, B) they're homos. No kids, no dogs, and a discount on furniture? Chances are they have a nice house.

Stereotypes can be annoying and hurtful, but they can also be funny and frankly, accurate.

I started writing this piece after I saw the TV show *Will & Grace* with my friend and my favourite character Jack McFarland came on. Now, okay, I *love* homos, and I *fucking love* Jack. Jack is the reason I love homos. I love everything about him from his annoying show-tunes attitude to his blatant ability to suck things out of his friends. Jack is my fucking hero.

I told that to my friend Jason and he said, "Jack's a fucking stereotype. I hate him. He's detrimental to gays' fight for equality. It's blatantly HOMOPHOBIC."

Sometimes I think we forget just how and why it sucks to be gay.

GAY SUCKS BECAUSE OTHER PEOPLE TREAT US SHITTY.
GAY DOES NOT SUCK BECAUSE OF WHO WE ARE.

Homophobia is a rock in the face because you're wearing your pride flag on your sleeve.

JACK, on the other hand, is a HOMO.

And you just know that he's always been a dancing, prancing homo. Probably he was a dancing, prancing homo in high school and grade school. And they all probably treated him shitty for it, made him play soccer and stuff when he clearly didn't want to. They probably gave him wedgies, they probably even called him a homo, and not with a swelling of pride in their hearts, like when I say it.

Maybe that's the most important reason to like homos, because despite the shittiness of the rest of society, they survived to be really cool people. It always amazes me that you don't see more homos on rooftops with rifles. You see the way most homos are treated in high school and you know they deserve the opportunity to vent their frustration. They have the right to do it but they don't, they go to the disco instead, sweat it out, and have sex.

And why not?

When they're all so terribly good-looking.

And they're such fabulous dancers.

Secretary 101

for Lisa Ayuso aka Tracey Remington

(The following speech was delivered at a Women Working For Very Little Money In Very Tight Suits Seminar at the Howard Johnson)

THE WORLD IS INDEED a strange place when someone like myself gets to be an authority on any kind of employment. I say this not in any kind of false modesty, believe me, but rather in light of the fact that I am probably the worst secretary that ever walked the face of the earth. If they sold pumps in packs of four, a seeing-eye dog would be a better secretary than I am now. A seeing-eye dog, you would hope, would at least be on time. I, throughout my career, have managed to arrive late and leave early every working day of my life. When someone suggested I give a speech about being a secretary I nearly choked on my Jolt. I mean, public masturbation, rug hooking, taxidermy, sure, but secretarial work? Come on! Why not focus on the stuff I can do?

At this point I asked myself the question that brought me here today:

"If you really suck at this job, why is it you've never been fired?"

Because, you know, I haven't. In all my years as a secretary and temp, despite my ineptitude, I have never been canned.

Why not?

The answer, to me, is clear. Apparently I am rather good at being a bad secretary. Good enough, at least, to get away with all my evil doings.

So without further ado, here are a few quick hints on how you too can be a very good bad secretary.

LESSON ONE: THE BASICS OF AVOIDING WORK
Your first challenge as a secretary is to avoid work. The two most important words in any secretary's life are "lunch break." If you're smart you can distil this down to one word: *break*. As in, "I have to take a *break*, I'm outta here."

There are ten to twenty valid reasons to go on a break. A decent secretary can think of at least 100. If you work for a man, the easiest breaks to pull off are bathroom breaks. It is a universal truth that men don't want to know a woman's reasons for going to the bathroom. If he asks, which he won't, but if for example it's your tenth time that morning, be up front and overly honest. The words "heavy menstrual flow," "lazy bladder," or "loose tampon," whispered while you discreetly cross your legs, will ensure that he won't ever bother you again with his petty questions. A loose tampon to a man in a suit is a loose cannon.

LESSON TWO: IF YOU BELIEVE IT, THEY WILL BUY IT
Overall, the best way to get anything as a secretary, be it a better office or a longer lunch, is to believe you need it. Bosses, especially corporate-sector bosses, are like bears: they have radar to detect fear, but they don't have radar to detect good acting. You can tell this by the fact that most of them are surprised when their spouses take off with half their money and the nanny. If you can convince yourself that you have to leave the office for an ice-cream cone because of a low blood-sugar level, you can convince your boss. Remember, some of the best secretaries are either hypochondriacs or really good at pretending they are.

LESSON THREE: OVERACT
When dealing with illness as a receptionist, more is never enough. Subtle will get you nowhere in an office full of people who don't want to be there. If you want something, specifically, if you want to leave, you have to be the

most compelling person in the room. Remember, the squeaky wheel gets the grease. Failing that, be the grossest. One of the best ways to get a sick leave is to threaten to push your illness on those around you. This doesn't mean coughing or sneezing on people: office types are usually squeamish enough that the mere threat of exposure to bodily fluids is enough. Probably one of the more successful stunts to pull if you want to get out early is the abscessed tooth. This practically always works, because due to the fact that no one wants to look at a pus-filled molar, no one really knows what one looks like. Casually leaning in to your boss and asking, "Does this look inflamed to you?" will get you out of the office in no time.

LESSON FOUR: SLEEP

Getting a good sleep while in the office will be your biggest challenge. Knowing that at some point you're going to fall asleep in the office (especially with the KISS FM they'll probably have on the radio), it's best to be prepared. Shortly after you are hired, pull your boss aside and confide — with a shade of shyness and embarrassment — that you have recently suffered the occasional fainting spell. Next, when you want to have a nap, and there's no one around, arrange yourself in a suitable collapsed position on the floor. Sprawled out just behind a door is good, I prefer the splayed-beside-the-overturned-chair, only because I think it suggests a little more dramatic flair. When your boss returns, wait for him or her to find you and wake you up. Remember, this won't work if you just pop up out of your coma as soon as your boss walks in the door. Recognize your limits as an actress. Be subtle, feign shock and surprise, rub your head, mumble. Some possible "just out of my coma" phrases you might want to try could be "Oh my God did I faint?" and the popular, "Where am I?" I usually lay it on a little thick with a couple of lines of "Dad?"

People ask me all the time if I ever feel bad about screwing over the people I work for. I guess, sometimes, at the end of the day, while carting home a couple hundred dollars' worth of office supplies in my knapsack, I do feel a little twinge of what you might call guilt. This despite the fact that my most recent contracts have been with big corporations that have little or no connection to worthwhile causes. Although the one time I did work for a charitable organization, the Canadian Prostate Cancer Research Foundation, I spent half my days whacking off in the bathroom and fiddling with my vibrator under my desk. Saving lives wasn't really on the top of my agenda even then. Maybe the truth is that I'm a sucker for a challenge. And while there might not be any challenge in doing secretarial work — even a fetus could answer a phone — there is a challenge in avoiding secretarial work, day after day after day.

My motto: They may not have hired you because you are smart. But you'll survive, and enjoy yourself doing so, because you are, at least, smarter than management.

Do You Practice Stupid Sex?

*

A GOOD FRIEND of mine once noted that in an age when having sex without a condom is opening your body to a lottery of potential disease, the thing that scares him the most about sex isn't disease at all, it's *people*. Tired of psychos and stalkers, starfuckers and the social nerds, he's throwing in the towel until he's married, which might be a really long time from now. My friend's decision is an interesting one when you consider the fact that we're often less concerned about sleeping with a psycho than we are about sleeping with a psycho without a condom. It all sounds very progressive until you consider all those people out there sleeping with potential stalkers.

This is not to say that we should pooh pooh the condom and the hour of sex education (per week) that we received in high school that focused on the condom as well as on the basics of sexual anatomy. It's an acquired and necessary skill to know how to slip a condom on a banana and locate your clitoris. Every time I or someone else finds my clitoris, I thank the Lord for the phys ed teachers who taught what in my school was referred to as "Health."

Still, my friend's decision made me think. Unfortunately, it seemed, though a high school education had taught him *how* to put on a condom, it had not prepared him for the decision of *who* to put a condom on. The big picture here involves not just the prevention of SAFE SEX, but the prevention of STUPID SEX, which can be just as damaging, but is a relatively ignored field in our society.

So, after much introspection, and despite the warning of my friend Jeff, who says the prevention of STUPID SEX is something you cannot learn from a book, here is a list of a few examples of stupid sexual activities. The smarter of you will note that not all of these activities actually involve having sex, a minor technicality since you don't actually have to have sex to make an ass of yourself (and look stupid).

1 SEX UNDER THE INFLUENCE

Usually happens in bars.

Usually happens with alcohol in bloodstream.

I wasn't actually going to consider this a category until my roommate, who is from Scarborough and very wise (a rare combination), made a startling point. "There's drunken sex," she noted, "and sex you would only have IF drunk." Super true. Incredibly unfortunate that it's so impossible to make that distinction, or any other, when you are drunk. I had a particularly nasty turn with this one once when I had drunken sex with someone who was considerably drunker than I was. Unbeknownst to me, she had spent a good portion of the evening making out with my ex before she ended up with me at my place. All this would have been okay, I think, if she hadn't thrown up all over my ex-girlfriend mere minutes before she went home with me. It was difficult to discern, at that point, who exactly had got the bad end of the stick on that particular evening, especially since I couldn't really remember how the sex was. *Nice.*

Several days later, a wise friend who had a penchant for bar stools and good conversation, gave me a sweet piece of advice I've kept by my side ever since. We were sitting on our stools around three in the morning when she turned and pointed at me.

"You smell that?" she asked.

"What?"

"You smell that? The beer and the CK One and the sweat?

That's desperation. If you're ever in a bar wandering around and you don't smell it, it's because you're desperate. Desperate people can never smell desperation. If you're ever in a bar at three o'clock and you can't smell it, you come and get me and I'll take you home… before you go home with someone more desperate than you… and regret it."

Who says the buddy system doesn't work?

I've often used it since.

2 SEX AS REVENGE

Usually happens with someone you will bump into on a regular basis for the rest of your life.

There is perhaps no worse way of getting revenge and no better way of acquiring a reputation as an asshole than having sex in an attempt to get revenge. It flat-out doesn't work. I know this because I tried it, several years ago, and it blew up in my face like so many cream pies.

Do I have to get into the details here?

I had a girlfriend, once, who was a total *slut* in a bad way. She was like sexual Jell-O constantly falling off my spoon and into the laps of all my friends. Literally. (The fact that this woman was an Environmental Studies major is probably the reason I still don't recycle.) One night, tired of watching her fondle my all-too-willing friends, I decided I'd had enough and went off and tried to seduce an anonymous dyke in glasses, hoping when the girl-friend in question saw me with someone else she would at least come and get me (take me home and stop touching my friends). Three beers and a brief make-out session later, I looked around and noticed that my girlfriend had *left* the bar *with* the boy. Furious and annoyed at both my own stupidity and the smuttiness of my girlfriend, I stomped home, bitter, drunk, and alone. The next day my girlfriend announced that in light of the previous night's events it was clear that what we needed was a non-monogamous relationship to suit both of our desires to see and be with other people. Refusing to 'fess up to the fact that I had been putting on a show to make her jealous, I agreed and she dated three more of my friends before we finally broke up (not because of that, mind you, but because I ate meat = whole other story).

I blamed the break up on her, but my friends know I carry a generous portion in the asshole element of that relationship. I am well aware that I am extremely lucky my anonymous dyke with glasses didn't have a bit of a penchant for revenge herself.

Bringing a third party into an angry sex triangle is like bringing a Bic to a meeting of pyromaniacs. Clearly, if you're in a position where someone you've slept with hates you, the last thing you need to do is sleep with more people.

3 SEX WITH YOUR ROOMMATE

Usually happens with: the best of intentions.

There comes a time in every woman's life where she just wants to get laid and, frankly, she doesn't really care how or with whom it happens. It's like when you're hungry and someone wants to know what you want to eat. *Anything!* Whether this happens because of ovulation, a recent break up, or alcohol (see #1) is rarely a concern because basically, when the deed is done and you're sitting around the next morning looking for your underwear before you get out of bed and dash out the door, it doesn't really matter *why* you did it. All that matters at · six o'clock in the morning is that you did *do it*, which makes you a stupid person.

Part of the problem, I think, is that we've temporarily replaced a *reality check* with *logic*, which is not, I must say, any kind of replacement. Logic, I always say, is like that stupid dance move you've been practicing in front of your mirror. Fine to practice it when you're at home alone (where little damage can be done — if you keep your shutters closed), quite another thing to take that dance move to the public.

In case you're still confused, let me give you a good example.

Logic says: OK, I'm really, really horny and so is my roommate. We totally respect each other, he's a really nice person, and I think we could sleep together once and be adult about it. He sleeps with people all the time. It's no big deal.

A *reality check* tells you: This is going to totally fuck things up. Roommates do not just have sex. COUPLES OR STRANGERS OR PEOPLE WHO DON'T LIVE TOGETHER HAVE SEX. NOT roommates.

I know of two roommates (with a lovely two-bedroom in the downtown area that had a garden and everything) who recently had to sell above-mentioned perfectly good house because they "took their dance moves to the public" after several beers, a rock show, and a recent breakup on her side. The next morning the sun rose in her little room like Armageddon. The inevitable happened, one week later he was in love with her and she was back in love with her boyfriend. They tried to stick it out for a month, then, both without telling the other, gave their notice.

There is no human litmus test for potential post-messing around weirdness and if there were, we'd probably ignore it.

4 SEX ON A CRUSH

Usually happens with someone who doesn't even know who you are.

A couple of years ago I made the overwhelming discovery that it is impossible to have sex *with* a crush. Just as you don't have a crush with someone (you have a crush *on* them), it's similarly impossible to have sex *with* a crush. To understand why, it is first necessary to understand that a crush, despite popular belief, is not a person with whom you can have sex. A crush is a fantasy, and a fantasy is impossible to get into bed because, well, they're not real. If we could have sex with a crush, considering all the crazy in love things we'd do to get into this position, it would probably be the best sex ever. My Catholic dyke friends, who are always coming up with bummer theories, suggest this is why it could never happen.

I'll use a story of my own embarrassment to illustrate. Several years ago when I was first coming out I fell in love with a social worker we'll call Jenny. Jenny was this beautiful butch with a social conscience and a heart of gold who saw me as both too young and really annoying. For reasons I cannot explain, this led me, one evening, to fall head over heels in *crush* with her. I remember distinctly that I was standing against a wall listening to Melissa Etheridge when it happened. The impact knocked the cigarette from my hand.

Sadly, as a young and inexperienced lesbian, I had only teenage heterosexual tactics in my arsenal to manipulate her. Accordingly, I invited myself along to several parties held at her house, got excessively drunk, and, at the end of each night, passed out on her couch. I was pathetically sure I was being so endearing that she would see my overwhelming desire for her and fall in love with me whilst placing cold towels on my forehead. Instead, Jenny told everyone I was an alcoholic. She invited me out on what I believed was a date and confronted me with my addiction, handing over a handful of AA pamphlets from her workplace.

I spent the rest of the evening looking for a sharp object with which to impale myself. Eventually, weeks later, after following her around campus and scouting out her favourite coffee spot, I confronted her over a cappuccino and told her I believed we were meant for each other.

"How is that," she said. "Mariko, you don't know anything about me."

That night I went home and, drunk on homemade margaritas, made a list of all the things I did know about Jenny. It wasn't a whole lot. Did that matter? In the end, several months later, it occurred to me that what did matter was not all the things I didn't know about Jenny, but all the things I assumed to know about her, having literally constructed a virtual personality for her during my intense crush.

A member of my poetry group, a year later, had a similar situation when she fell in *crush* with a boy in her Social Problems class and followed him around for several weeks. Crushes are the clearest illustration of how sexual attraction makes people crazy. This particular friend even took the precaution of getting a calling card (a trick I taught her) so she could anonymously call him from pay phones to see if he was home (call display). Eventually she worked her way into his group of friends and started getting invited to parties where he would be. One night, on Halloween, she dressed up as a fairy princess and managed to seduce him. He took her into the bathroom and they had sex with her little fairy costume still tied around her waist. Two weeks later my friend was in the bitter end part of the crush experience, sitting at home by the phone and waiting for the guy who did you in the bathroom to call. For anyone who's looking, this is a really good way to lose weight and save money, because you can't eat and you never go out. Other than that, the experience basically bites the big one. From then on she wrote a lot of angry poems about fairies and never had sex with her clothes on. Having a crush doesn't necessarily mean you're going to have stupid sex. I have another friend who masturbates to dreams of her crushes but never sleeps with them. I asked her why once and she said that her masturbation fantasies last about three minutes.

"There's no way you can fit a whole personality in there," she said, "at the most you fit like maybe a smile in. Real personalities take up a lifetime. If I'm going to have sex with someone it won't be because of some two-minute fantasy, it will be because I know the real person."

5 SEX WITH A STAR

Usually happens with small "c" celebrities (anyone who has a show on the CBC, anyone who's ever been on the Comedy Network, anyone who's ever been published).

It's tough, I realize, to apply this kind of reality check when dealing with celebrities and sex. There's something bright and shiny about celebrities, even small "c" celebrities, that affects the people around them. It's almost impossible to be around someone famous and not want to impress them somehow, whether by making them laugh, making them smile, or, ultimately, making them scream out your name.

Unfortunately, despite popular belief, fame is less of a Joseph's Coat of Many Colours and more of a red T-shirt. Unlike the Coat of Many Colours, which comes with a cool dude guarantee, you can have a red T-shirt and be amazing in bed, and you can have a red T-shirt and be an asshole. (While we're on the subject, I once almost slept with someone because they had these unbelievable shoes until this other friend came up to me and said, "Mariko, don't be stupid, I have those shoes.") I was talking to my friend Jennifer about celebrity sex and she told me about this comedian she slept with (no names) who seemed really great (i.e., funny) until it turned out he could only get off if he did her from behind with her pulling his balls and laughing at his jokes. This is not the only weird and messed-up starfuck story I've ever heard, which makes me wonder if there is some kind of special celebrity sex.

I should point out something else here. While it is not stupid to have sex with someone who happens to be famous, it IS stupid to have sex with someone because they're famous. Another thing to consider, with celebrities, is that rarely, in celebrity biographies, do you hear glowing reviews of how celebrity x was in bed. What you do hear, however, is scandal, and scandal is neither fun, nor sexy, nor suggestive of any intelligence on your part. (Do YOU think the people that appear in celebrity biographies and the tabloids are smart? Me neither.)

Just so you all don't feel too bad, I'd like to end this story with an extreme example that will make everyone feel better about all the weird things they've done.

A couple of weeks ago I had a conversation with a friend I have in New York who does a performance/slide show featuring a series of different things people put in their assholes. On that day, after the show, someone had approached her and told her about an incident he'd had at an emergency room several weeks before. Apparently, one night he'd been playing with a particular toy and it disappeared up his ass. He went to the emergency room and had it removed, they gave him his toy back, and he went home. Several hours later he returned to the same ER with the same toy stuck up his ass, and this time, when they removed it, they refused to give it back to him.

"Can they do that?" the man asked her, somewhat incensed. This, for me, is a prime example of the one and only real golden rule of non-stupid sex, which is: YOU MUST LEARN FROM YOUR MISTAKES.

While it is perfectly okay to screw up and go home with someone who will make your life a living hell for the next two months, it totally isn't okay to turn around three months later and do it again. There, I think, you cross the boundary from having stupid sex to being a stupid person. What's the difference between the two? Two things: time and the ability to absorb information. Learn from my mistakes, if you want, learn from your friends', and, if you absolutely have to, learn from your own.

The Epil-Lady vs.
The Hairy Asian

*

A COUPLE OF DAYS ago a woman came into the sex-toy store where I work looking for love in all the wrong places. She was in Toronto on a brief vacation and was trying to put an orgy together with an excess of enthusiasm and one day's notice. Good luck, I told her. This is Toronto, the only things that happen on a day's notice here are large purchases and bank loans. Torontonians talk big but we're mostly a city of tall buildings and big hype. Even really good-looking people have trouble getting things done here, especially in the winter.

This woman was from Italy, with tall black hair that looked like two gloved hands poking out either side of her skull. She was appropriately long and thin, dressed in an unwrinkled white linen dress sprinkled with black dots like a really expensive domino. Her arms were loaded down with two great paper wings of shopping bags that she was scattering around the store as she hunted for the perfect butt plug and other accessories. She wasn't even looking at the price tags as she piled up her potential purchases and chatted endlessly about her dream orgy. I have this crazy snob reflex that kicks in and makes me very accommodating when I see someone's about to buy more than $300 worth of stuff. I was also, I admit, completely obsessed with these bracelets I had noticed on this woman's arms. They were like tiny little tiaras. Incredible.

I took a long moment to ponder whether or not it was worth participating in this little orgy, if only so that I could wake up early in the morning and snag the bracelet off this woman as she lay sleeping. I think sleeping with strangers for souvenirs is immature, but I do it all the time.

In the end I didn't sleep with her, not because I didn't really like those bracelets but because, it turned out, she wouldn't sleep with me. Before I could even bat my eyelashes she had me sized up.

As we stood in front of the S/M section she grabbed my arm and cooed at me. "Oh, you know," she said, "I love Asians, so beautiful and exotic. Really, normally I love

Asians. The only thing I don't like, I think, is the hairy Asians." As she said this she gave me a long look up and down my body and quietly shook her head.

Now, I have been turned down in the past. I have also had the experience of being turned down before I even get a chance to show the slightest bit of interest. But I have never, in my life, been called a hairy Asian.

I'm not going to be defensive here but I am also not exactly what I would call excessively hairy. As a dyke I have seen my share of fuzzy legs and bushy pits and I can tell you that my own crop of hair pales in comparison with what you'll find at your local YMCA. Beyond this I should add that I think a little bit of fur can be sexy so my own treasure trail doesn't bother me.

As we continued our conversation, however, I noticed that this woman had absolutely no body hair. It was a strange thing to notice, kind of the opposite of seeing the mirage of a puddle on the road only to realize it's just the sun hitting the asphalt. I just thought she was really tan. Looking closer I saw that her arms and legs were uniformly golden brown from the tip of her fingers to even the fine skin under her arms. They were almost shiny like Barbie arms.

"Oh, it's all gone," she chuckled, noticing my stare. "Every single dirty hair. So unhygienic. I get rid of it all every week with my Epilady."

"Wow," I said, as she held out her arm for me to feel. It felt a little like touching the underside of a frog's belly.

Now, for those of you who don't know, an Epilady is probably one of the most innocuous-looking and yet entirely deadly inventions to ever grace the Sears catalog. Basically, it's a hair-removal system that consists of a mechanical twisting metal coil that RIPS the hair out of a woman's body by the root. Once, ONCE, I let someone go at me with one of these things at summer camp. It felt like someone was twisting hot metal screws into my thigh. Anyone who tells you that this thing isn't *extremely* painful is a liar who doesn't like you very much so BE-WARE.

"Wow," I said again to the Epil-Lady.

At this point I was kind of expecting her to go off on her own and leave me alone. I was, after all, not only very busy but also, as we had both acknowledged, too hairy. Apparently, the hairless woman was not exactly done with me.

"All of it," she whispered, leaning into me a bit, "even got rid of the hair back there."

"On your back?" I asked.

"Oh no, no, no," she chucked. "No, I mean IN back there, around my anus."

Now I have only worked in the sex-toy business for a while and I have heard a lot of different things in the meantime. I once spent an afternoon wrapping and rewrapping my friend in Saran Wrap and inserting little microphones into her belly button so she could do a performance piece on the audio-reactive suggestion. I once painted some guy's ass with a million little happy faces in a bar as part of a fundraiser. So don't call me squeamish. But the thought of this woman reaching back to yank the hairs out of her asshole with her Epilady got me this close to passing out right there on the floor of the store. I did my very best to keep a pleasant smile on my face as I rang up the rest of her purchases.

In the end, the woman did invite me to her orgy, suggesting that I might let her take a go at the hair on my arms with her Epilady. I gave the number to a bunch of hairy field-hockey lesbians I knew instead, none of whom I've heard from since.

Hey, I thought to myself as I lounged on the couch in all my hairiness that night, there are some things we won't do for jewellery. Not many but some.

Almost Sex

Let us first agree that, somewhere, out there, in the Greater Toronto Area, there is a woman who is in bed with another woman.

This lucky woman, in bed with another woman, is in the throes of what will pass for sexual ecstasy, which you can tell immediately because she's a bit of a screamer. She's also a bit of a control freak, who is keeping a mental tab of where her underwear landed so she can find it later. It is not her house, so she's worried about losing her underwear.

Let's say, without judgement, that she's a bit of a slut, and she does this a lot, and she can't afford to lose any more undies.

So she's keeping tabs.

Another thing this woman, whom we will call Lucy, is doing is thinking about several things.

She can do this because Lucy's a lesbian and lesbians are classic multi-taskers.

Lucy is noting that it's 7 p.m., that the moon is in its second quarter, that she is therefore eight days away from her menstrual period, that her partner is good-looking, maybe *very* good-looking, that the furniture in this apartment is largely from IKEA, although the vase on the bedside table looks like it might be from Martha Stewart.com.

Unfortunately, of all the things that are occurring to Lucy, the one thing that probably hasn't and won't is that she, Lucy, might not be having sex.

Yes, ladies and other interested parties. Despite the fact that she is in bed with another woman doing stuff, the other woman doing stuff as well, and despite the fact that Lucy believes that she is having sex, she might in fact be in bed with a woman who thinks… who will later tell her… that what they are doing is not sex.

Almost sex.

But not sex.

It could be happening right now.

The only comforting thing about this whole scenario is that it's happening to Lucy and not me.

Not that it would be a surprise if it were me.

It's just not me tonight.

To begin with, my humble introduction to almost sex began when I was an ugly fourteen-year-old girl at a private school in uptown Toronto.

The thing is, as you who have been ugly teenagers or have at least watched any film by John Hughes will know, the problem with being an ugly teenager is that it's incredibly hard to get laid.

Technically, of course, since all teenagers are ugly, this shouldn't be a problem.

But it is.

Interestingly enough, though it is hard for an ugly teenage girl to have sex it's not all that hard for her, that is me, the old me, to almost have sex. All you have to do to almost have sex is get on the dance floor. It's sad to say that the only place to find real equal opportunity was in a barely lit gymnasium, but it is definitely true.

You could be a three-headed monster with a face full of acne on a dimly lit dance floor, it didn't matter so long as you were a slutty three-headed monster with a face full of acne.

Suffice it to say that for the majority of my high school sex life, the running man was foreplay.

I've tried to think of some way to describe for you what happened in those dark and dusty corners while I was tangled with various anonymous boys (one at a time of course) from Upper Canada College. When they hear me describe this, people usually have varying reactions depending on whether they picture us sitting or standing. I usually stood so I could avoid getting my ass dusty. You could still do a lot this way, you just had to lean a little. What exactly did we do? The best analogy I can think of is that it was like the time my parents allowed me to play in the car and I pretended to drive but I didn't have any keys. Essentially I could grab the stick but I couldn't really GO anywhere with it.

Like that.

Whatever I did, it was always over by the time "Stairway to Heaven" came on, a song I still associate with the sound of hastily zipped zippers. When you're fourteen and in private school, almost sex ends with the sight of your latest conquest driving off in his parents' minivan.

I had a conversation with one of these boys shortly after I returned to Toronto. It started out as one of those, "Hey, how are you, back in Toronto I see… " discussions and quickly, perhaps too quickly, became one of those "Hey, didn't we have sex?" type conversations.

"No," I said, "I'm fairly sure we didn't. I remember those particular guys and you aren't one of them."

"Oh but we did," he said, "*didn't* we?"

Which made me wonder if at that age it's all just a blur of skin interrupted by nipples and body hair.

I mentioned this to a lesbian friend of mine and her response was a short, "Men," which, if you don't speak lesbian, means, "Ahhh we lesbians are so much smarter, nay, developed, than our hetero counterparts, are we not?"

As in, not like that would ever happen to a SISTER, right?

Ironically, this brings us back up to date with the leading cause of almost sex in the universe, which is not ugly teenagers, but lesbians.

As Lucy can attest to.

Now you wouldn't think this to be true because lesbians and ugly teenagers are supposed to be very different entities. Ugly teenagers are, of course, swathed in silence and self-loathing. They don't have a parade of any kind, they're not largely recognized as having any kind of particular skill, like social work or academia. In fact, in many ways, teenagers are kind of like pre-lesbians; this metaphor is kind of a stretch but it involves a kind of fumbling around in a dark, closet-like existence.

Lesbians on the other hand are evolved beings who write poetry and organize marches. We're in touch with our bodies, unlike ugly teenagers, and participate in body-painting type activities that involve nudity and often, more parades.

You can understand why almost sex would happen to teenagers, even pretty teenagers, because, well, they're sort of at the beginning of the race, aren't they? They don't know what to expect or even what they *can* expect. They're just starting to talk about sex... vague discussions that mostly involve the phrase, "Can we?"

Lesbians, on the other hand, are supposed to talk all the time, endlessly discussing and re-discussing and rhyming and putting to music. We're always talking about sex. We paint about sex, huge vaginas that we give to our friends to hang up in their living rooms. We write long and involved papers on symbolism and political context... sometimes for a living.

Aren't we supposed to be on top of this?

Maybe not.

Maybe, when you really think about it, there's one thing we're not doing in all this, which is clarifying, or defining, exactly what lesbian sex *is*.

Or at least, perhaps, what it *isn't*.

And before you get all defensive here, let me say that clearly we *do* have sex. Whenever straight people ask us what it is we *do* in bed, we're offended because, obviously, what we do in bed is have *sex*.

Right?

Unfortunately this does not explain the plight of women like Lucy, like me, and like every other dyke I know, who at one time or another has ended up having almost sex when they thought they were having sex.

In case you were wondering, this is infinitely more frustrating than the high school situation I described earlier, because at least with the high school situation you were a) just a teenager and b) supposed to be blinded by unstable hormone levels that excused you from keeping track of certain things.

I've had a night of passion that ended with a particularly disturbing conversation where I was told that what I was doing was not sex but in fact the practice of MUTUAL MASTURBATION.

"Just mutual masturbation?"

"Yes. Why, is there something wrong with that? You have something against masturbation?"

"No. I mean, technically no. Hey, wouldn't we have to agree that it was masturbation for it to be, you know, masturbation?"

"No."

"Are you sure?"

"Yes."

"So we ALMOST had sex."

"Sort of."

Now I am not one to haggle over definitions, by far. I went to university, okay, I had a book on semiotics. I'm an artist, for christsakes, I understand the value of the grey road between extremes.

But sometimes, boy, what you're doing on that road is SEX and it is sooooo frustrating to get off that road and have someone tell you it can't be sex because you were in a car. Like you can't have sex in a car; what is that? It's a blatant lack of imagination is what it is.

I've tried to come up with some solution to this problem and the only thing I can think of is that we, lesbians, as hard as this is to believe, are going to have to beef up our communication skills. And what this really means is that we're going to have to talk more during sex. This might involve something as simple as asking, "So, are we having sex now?" at various points in the evening.

Another friend of mine suggested a system where you both agree to drop your bra on the floor when you think you're actually having sex. You might feel stupid but at least you'll know what you're doing, which we all know is of infinite importance.

The other option, of course, is to take a broader view of the situation and decide that ultimately, whether or not you are having sex, you are still enjoying yourself, and the interaction, however it might be defined, has some sort of intrinsic value. Whatever works for you is fine. I, myself, will be doing the bra hitting the floor thing from now on.

Just so you know.

Titanic

*

DID YOU EVER fall in love with a wreck?

That boy/girl you knew was a disaster waiting to happen, but fell in love with anyway?

Did you ever fall in love with a mistake?

A beautiful mistake?

Maybe you noticed her from across a crowded room, saw the barbed wire and tire tracks snaking up and down her back?

Maybe it was your first date, and you'd already run into two angry exes, at two separate bars, and she sat you down to give you a hickey and tell you about her passion for broken glass and making people cry?

Go home with her. You might as well. You're not the first and you won't be the last.

We're all mesmerized, hating to look but looking anyway on the highway, stopping traffic because there's a little piece of all of us that loves the idea of an accident.

That's why we call them when our friends tear their hair out, shake their heads, and swear up and down they won't be a shoulder to cry on.

We're stupid.

We're in love.

I have a friend who ended up in the hospital once after moving in with a woman who had eight cats. She was allergic, but unfortunately, in love, so she unpacked her things and said nothing. She bought a lint brush and made a futile effort to keep the hair and dander that was killing her at bay. Every day it got harder and harder to breathe until one evening, during a potluck and Susan Sarandon filmfest, she passed out and fell down the stairs. Later, at the hospital, she admitted her secret to her lover.

"Oh I knew that," her girlfriend said, "but I thought you were doing okay."

They're still together.

The things we do for love.

The things we do to the people we love.

I had a girlfriend once named Marsha who was drawn to disaster, willingly and knowingly. She was the worst kind of masochist, pulled towards broken hearts and drama, a lover of soap operas and the idea of having a life that lived like a soap opera (and here, of course, we're referring to American soap operas, which are much more extravagant and gaudy than their British counterparts and, hence, more alluring). Before me, Marsha dated a serial heartbreaker named Soooz. Soooz was one of those long, slinky creatures who fits into everything that people like me usually don't like. I mean, her name was Soooz... "SOOOOOZ"... it sounds like sex no matter what your feelings are on the matter. What kind of unfair advantage is that?

Soooz was a predictably slippery creature who liked to bring strange men home and sleep with them in the living room. Marsha would wake up in the morning to make coffee and find them tangled on her couch.

"It's just physical," Soooz would tell her.

I got together with Marsha the night she broke up with Soooz at a Valentine's Day party gone horribly wrong. Marsha was dressed as a bride and Soooz was supposed to be the groom, but instead she showed up with a groom, a tall man in a tuxedo, clearly anxious to take up a position on the living-room couch. Maybe it was because it was a party, a place to make a scene, Marsha hiked up her huge white dress and kicked Soooz out the door with her white sequined boots. Then she ran upstairs to the balcony to pelt Soooz and the boy with wine bottles which resulted in a street littered with green glass.

I still think that the only reason Marsha ever slept with me was because at the time, I had a black eye (which was actually from tripping and hitting my face on the corner of my desk) and I was dressed as Joan of Arc. She found me in the bathroom trying to get a red-wine stain off my dress and pushed me into the bathtub.

In the end, I wasn't a catastrophe, though it was not for lack of trying. It's hard to be a catastrophe when really you're just a manic-depressive with a bit of a bad shopping habit. Marsha left me to run off to Seattle to date musicians (who are always in one mess or another).

She left a note that said, "Call me if you're ever in trouble."

Last week I went and saw a play by a famous gay Torontonian playwright (famous because he was from Toronto, not because he was gay) about a lonely homosexual who's told, on the day of his thirteenth birthday, that on the day he falls in love he will be struck down by a meteor from heaven. Not wanting to be struck by falling rock, or to have anyone else struck by falling rock, the man vows celibacy, and goes into teaching. (Somehow those last two things are supposed to relate.) Eventually, though, the homosexual falls in love with another homosexual and they are both killed at a parent/teacher picnic for the school at Algonquin Park.

The moral of the play, one would guess from the ending, is that man must ultimately learn to overcome his fears (of love, intimacy, death, and the future). The play is called: ONLY _ _ _ _ MATTERS.

I hated it, not because it was two and a half hours long, or because it took place in Algonquin Park, or even because it was bad (another play/movie about doomed people finding love). What bothered me was that the doomed homosexual never tells his lover that they're doomed. He just invites him to the picnic and then cops this tremendous feel behind the port-a-potties. It's not supposed to matter because they're in love.

But I can't help but think that if I was going to be struck by a falling meteor, I'd want the option of an informed decision to put myself in that position.

I interviewed the playwright after and he said it was a metaphor for AIDS. "Oh."

I told him about my big gripe and he smiled.

"You can't be told," he said, "that you're walking into a disaster. You have to find out for yourself."

Plus, he said, there was some sort of beauty to disaster. Wasn't Saint Valentine, a tragic character whose name and words would forever be associated with love, beaten and beheaded?

"Trust me," he said, "if you want to be a writer you're going to have to get used to catastrophe and disaster."

Just make sure you always remember to write it all down.

Confessions of a Girl Who Is Not a Big Fan of BDSM

*

YOU SHOULD KNOW, before you judge my opinion of sado-masochism (which is not, I have to say, a good one), that I was not always the tame, mild-mannered individual you see before you.

I used to live in Montreal.

I used to live in Montreal in cheap Montreal apartments that were crawling with overly idealistic experimenting teenagers. I used to live in Montreal where I was an overly idealistic and experimenting teenager. I used to fuck Montrealers, or at least people originally from

Toronto who were living in Montreal attending McGill or Concordia University. Women who zestfully, if drunkenly, tied me to the roof of my apartment with vintage leather belts and recently purchased, often only decorative, leather cuffs at three o'clock in the morning to flog me with strings of plastic pearls.

I used to say stuff like, "Yeah I'd LIKE to sit down, but the welts from my dungeon session last night are still sore so I'll just stand and drink instead."

All of this can be counted against what I am about to say about the community I once, though perhaps mistakenly, considered myself a part of.

I mention this because of my friend Jerri, a dominatrix/accountant with whom I recently had an extended conversation over coffee and expensive pastries. Jerri thinks I am a BDSM-phobe, which essentially, she says, means I am afraid of what I don't understand.

Jerri is of the opinion that I am the kind of person who can't deal with complications and contradictions, which, she says, is what BDSM is all about.

That and fashion.

She's mad because I recently started boycotting her parties, coming up with flimsy and obvious excuses for my absence. Jerri's parties (basically all of Jerri's parties) are S/M events, black-lighting affairs with wall-to-wall bondage leather fanatics, a lot of people taking themselves way too seriously and shifting their harnesses so they don't pinch the skin. FUN. I told this to Jerri and she turned it into a whole You Just Don't Understand Me Bit, something frequently used by both the BDSM and artistic communities.

Jerri and I have had the argument before where she insists that the BDSM community and artistic community are closely linked, both hovering on the outskirts of society, constantly challenging its assumptions by pushing its boundaries.

I'm more inclined to see a link between BDSM enthusiasts and drag queens, both of which groups are free to live a relatively artistic and bohemian lifestyle (challenging society's assumptions, etc.), complete with perks like periodic bouts of emotional upheaval and dramatic fits, without the actual responsibility of producing any art.

Granted, I know one or two dominatrixes (some of whom might throw great parties) who can tie a knot like no one's business, creating intricate braziers with elbow grease and a little bit of string. That I think is an art form, but I also know a lot of leather boys and girls who act like they've just written an opera every time they spank someone's ass.

I suppose you could say there are also a lot of writers and artists out there who take a huge bite of credit for a little nibble of work. I would agree and say that I don't like going to their parties either.

Secretly, the main reason I'm not going to Jerri's parties any more is that her parties are ruining my friends. Every time I bring a friend to one of Jerri's stupid parties, he or she ends up sleeping with her and getting all into her little world of pain and power; it kills me.

Take my latest disaster, David, who was once a perfectly nice boy from Scarborough, mild-mannered with a penchant for video games and Mel Gibson or Goldie Hawn films. David the innocent, whose only real concession to a wild side was a pair of pleather pants until he went to Jerri's Halloween party last year (everyone was dressed as a vampire, big surprise!) and ended up falling in love with her.

I take responsibility because technically I should have been looking after him, but was unfortunately under the influence of a recent breakup and this incredible whiskey that tastes like cinnamon hearts. Apparently, some time around midnight, Jerri took David under her cape and into her room, where she beat him on the bare ass with a hairbrush for three hours or something.

Whatever.

David said he saw the light.

Three months later and already David is borderline Mr. Leather and Pain 2001. He went out and bought all this gear and all he wants to talk about now is his experience of s/m. Having a conversation with David is like watching a soap opera where everyone repeats the same damn information over and over again super-grandpa style.

Or like talking to born-again Christians where every five minutes the conversation turns back to…

"So have we talked about Jesus yet?"

YES!

Once we went out and he got his fingers caught in the swinging door of a garbage can at McDonald's and in the parking lot, of all places, he started this long drawn-out diatribe about PAIN. For the next hour all he could talk about was the PAIN.

The cleansing pain.

The beauty of pain.

How pain is like power.

Blah

     Blah

       Blah

It's statements like these, and the one he made last week when he quit his job, that make me wonder if I shouldn't just put David out of his misery and stab him.

"If my experience with BDSM has taught me anything," he said, "it's taught me that LIFE is all about power."

The thing about this kind of statement is that they make it sound like the *only* way to learn that life is all about power is to have some dude in leather underwear go at you with a riding crop. Like there aren't a million other ways to learn these lessons. Like he knows some sort of secret code or something.

Hearing these little life lessons from David was like

hearing it from my parents, only a little bit worse because the person telling me this is wearing one of those ridiculous body harnesses.

The next night we were supposed to go dancing and he was two hours late because he had to go home and change his shirt, which wouldn't have been so bad, but he also had this incredibly smug smile on his face.

"My back was bleeding and sticking to my shirt," he said. "Really intense session with Raven."

Me: "Raven? Like the poem?"

"Like the bird."

For the next three hours all he could talk about was the pain. It was like walking around the park with a bunch of teenagers on acid.

"It's like, I can see things, like, differently, you know?"

I slapped him on the back and took off to the sound of him yelling, "Hey that was a total violation you know!"

Which is why we're kind of not talking any more.

I told this to my friend Louise, who also used to toy with leather boys in Montreal but who is now engaged to a loving vegan who also happens to be allergic to latex. She suggested that my biggest problem with BDSM is that I can't stand anyone taking anything seriously.

"As a dyke living amongst a community of vegans, Wiccans, divas, and dominatrixes," she said, "you might want to consider a practice of tolerance rather than criticism."

She might be right.

Jerri, certainly, thinks that this would be a good idea, although even she's not talking to David any more.

"That whore," she told me, "is letting Raven dominate him now. Bastard. Hope he knows that all of Raven's slaves are getting her dog's rash!"

Which makes me wonder if David will think rashes are as cool and mind-expanding as pain. It also makes me wonder when city life, in Toronto no less, became so sordid and complicated.

Dear Ms. Tamaki,

ON BEHALF OF the Writers' Guild of Canada
I'm afraid that I must officially request
that you cease referring to yourself as a writer
from this point forward.
We have,
at the request of several of your peers,
done an informal investigation
and discovered
that you have had
neither a disruptive childhood
nor an ounce of artistic integrity.

It was also revealed to us
by a private source
that you spent your grant money on shoes
and chips at the 7/11.

You have been heard
at recent gatherings
making fun of Margaret Atwood
and expressing an interest
in moving to the United States;
if you were an actor
this might be appropriate
but as a writer
this behaviour
borders on sacrilegious.
Move to Europe,
maybe,
but not the States.
I mean,
really.

We had hoped
that your homosexuality
and apparent disregard
for societal norms
would prove fruitful
but apparently
your apathy
and materialism
outweigh any potential these features might have offered.

Please return
your notebooks
(we know you have them stashed under your bed)
your air of superiority
and your caffeine addiction.

You can keep the computer
you only use it to surf the Web anyway.

We hope
you find some other way to serve your country
in another field
perhaps customer service
or family law.
We realize your prior plans
of becoming a marine biologist
are now out of the question
but are confident
you will find something else
to fill your time.

Yours sincerely,
The Writers' Guild of Canada

Mariko Tamaki is a writer, performer and actor. She has appeared on CBC Radio's "This Morning" and in Queeruption in New York City.

Other publications by Tamaki: *Cover Me* (McGilligan, 2000); "Angry Naked Fat Woman" in *Fireweed* Magazine (Issue #67, 1999); and "Do You Practice Stupid Sex?" in *Blood and Aphorisms* (Issue #40, 2000).

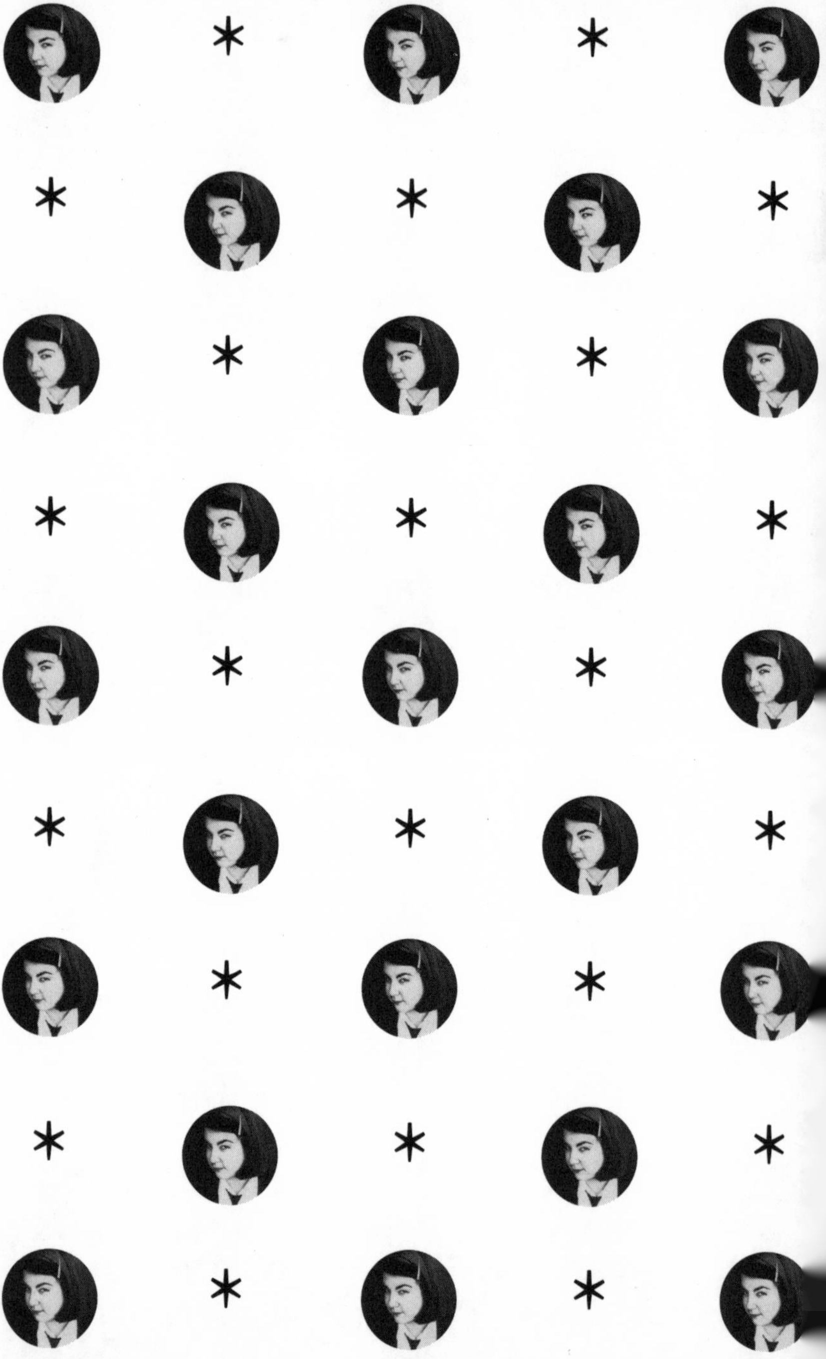